I looked over the edge of the ravine to see somebody there, helpless, barely moving. She lifted her head to look at me and I fled, stumbling, back to my room in Mr. Thiel's house.

Something had followed me there. Something, somebody, tall and dark, wrapped in a cloak, able to move soundlessly through the house.

He stood beside my bed. He pulled down the bedclothes. I wept and silently begged him to go away. She was still back there in the ravine, I knew that. I wanted him to go and help her.

He did not speak, but motioned with his arm to me. I was helpless. I was afraid. I did not know him. But he knew about the woman in the pool beneath the falls. The hood of his cloak hid his face in shadows . . .

Fawcett Juniper Books
by Cynthia Voigt

DICEY'S SONG
HOMECOMING
TELL ME IF THE LOVERS ARE LOSERS

THE
CALLENDER PAPERS

Cynthia Voigt

FAWCETT JUNIPER • NEW YORK

RLI: $\dfrac{\text{VL: 6 + up}}{\text{IL: 7 + up}}$

A Fawcett Juniper Book
Published by Ballantine Books

Library of Congress Catalog Card Number: 82-13797

ISBN 0-449-70078-X

This edition published by arrangement with Atheneum

Manufactured in the United States of America

First Ballantine Books Edition: August 1984
Second Printing: December 1984

Für Clara: eine kleine Gothik

Chapter One

*T*hink carefully was the guiding principle of my upbringing, spoken in Aunt Constance's firm voice. When I complained to her that the Latin mistress was stricter with me than with the other girls in the class, she would advise me, "Think carefully, Jean, before you become disheartened." When I balked at eating bean soup, at which I felt my stomach might revolt, she asked gently, "If you think carefully, would you choose to have your stomach govern your will?" When I criticized the students at the Wainwright Academy for quarreling so among themselves, she did not smile. "There are so few choices that a female can make, and those so crucial to her well-being—you would be wiser to understand than to disdain. Think carefully, Jean. These girls now are playing at making choices, which is one of the things we hope to teach here. From such quarrels they can learn about that strange, hidden thing, the heart. When a woman chooses a man to marry, she puts her life into his hands. When she chooses not to marry, she must be ready to put her life into her own hands. These quarrels are petty and tiresome, I grant you that, but there is something to be learned in them. They have a use."

I could not but agree with Aunt Constance. I agreed with her even if I sometimes inwardly rebelled against her strong, calm influence and felt myself quite able to think for myself. More than anything else I loved and admired Aunt Constance. Moreover, I had good reason to be grateful to her. This I *had* thought out for myself, because she never brought the subject up.

Although I shared her surname, I always knew that Miss Constance Wainwright was no blood relation. I cannot remember a time when I did not know this. Neither can I remember anything of my earlier life, which is not surprising when you think of it. "You were a babe in arms," Aunt Constance often told me, "a babe put into my arms. I thought you would prove companionable, so I undertook to raise you." About my parents she told me nothing, and I did not trouble her with questions. I knew that she would tell me, if she knew, and if it were for the best that I know. I never thought about my mother. Why should I? Aunt Constance was all the mother any child would need. She was also a dear friend and a stern teacher. To tell the truth, I never considered my orphaned state. I considered myself the niece of Miss Constance Wainwright, and fortunate to be in her care.

None of that feeling was altered by the events of that unsettling summer of 1894, which changed so much else in my life. I was going on thirteen that summer. The story actually began many years earlier, as I learned. But my part of it, my own part, commenced on a clear Saturday morning in April.

On that morning, Aunt Constance sent for me. I had been

outside, working in the kitchen garden, so I had to wash and put on a fresh apron before going to her. I hurried. It was unusual, even rare, for Aunt Constance to call for me on Saturdays. During the week I was kept busy with school-work and my responsibilities for the younger children. Therefore, on Saturdays I was left alone to do as I wished, as long as I appeared promptly for meals. On spring mornings I usually worked in the gardens, and in the afternoons I walked through Cambridge.

When I was presentable, I knocked on the door to Aunt Constance's office. "Enter," she said. She was sitting behind her big oak desk, looking every bit the headmistress she was, strict and fair-minded. She was in her mid-forties at that time, but her dark hair had little gray in it. The gray was in her plain taffeta dress and in her eyes. She was a handsome woman, her figure tall and straight; she had even features, and eyes that seemed to see right to the heart of things, especially of people. She smiled at me, and her whole face lighted with that. Beneath her sternness, Aunt Constance had a loving nature, as I had good reason to know. "Jean," she said. "Come in. You were working in the garden?"

"Yes." I held out my hand, where traces of dirt lingered around the edge of my nails. "I was turning the soil over again. We might plant next week, if the weather holds."

"Well, I won't keep you long. Do you recall Mr. Thiel?"

"Vividly," I said. He was one of the Governors of the Academy, and a generous patron. He was also an ill-tempered, impatient man, a man who had no difficulty saying exactly what he thought, and who, consequently, did not get along well with people. He dined with us once or twice a year and seemed to enjoy arguing with Aunt Constance. I must admit I also enjoyed those dinners. Mr. Thiel ignored me, although every now and then I would look up from my plate and catch him glaring at me. But it was Aunt Constance whose conversation he sought. He talked back to Aunt Constance, as nobody else dared. She spoke sharply to him, giving her vigorous mind full play. Their meetings were always interesting.

"He has written me a letter." Aunt Constance pointed to a piece of paper.

"Has he proposed?" I asked. (For some reason, I was determined that Mr. Thiel had designs on Aunt Constance. Why else should he make such large donations to her school but refuse to attend meetings of the Board of Governors? Why else should he take obvious, if quarrelsome, pleasure in dining with her?)

"Not that I noticed," Aunt Constance answered. "It's even more unexpected than that. See what you think of it."

The letter was succinct, and direct:

My Dear Miss Wainwright,

As you know, I have lived many years with an attic that holds endless Callender memorabilia and reams of unsorted Callender papers. My conscience gnaws at me. The material must be examined before it can be destroyed. I cannot bring myself to undertake the tedious task.

Have you a person who might be capable of dealing with this? A young man would, of course, be best, for Propriety. However, since your establishment allows none of that sex—due to your obstinate opinions—perhaps you have a female who might serve. She must be young, because a girl of eligible years would cause talk here in Marlborough. She should be familiar with some languages and be able to make decisions on her own. (I will not be unduly bothered by this task.) She must be reliable, energetic, unobtrusive, solitary, independent of mind, sensible and straightforward. Is there any such creature? I think of your odd little niece.

The salary I offer will be fair, the accommodations chaperoned by Mrs. Bywall.

D. Thiel

"Well," I said, returning the letter to Aunt Constance.

"Well," she answered, looking at me.

I quoted Aunt Constance's rule to her. "We must think carefully about this."

"Indeed we must. It is an unusual opportunity for a child of your age."

"That I am sure of."

Aunt Constance folded her hands on her desk. "Mr. Thiel would find you most satisfactory," she said.

"A salary would be useful, for Mt. Holyoke Seminary," I continued. That was my ambition: to study at the seminary, then return to the Wainwright Academy to teach and, ultimately, if I was worthy, become headmistress. It was a plan of which Aunt Constance had approved. "But I don't understand why Mr. Thiel asked particularly about me."

"He has his reasons, you can be sure of that."

"A child requires less food and less salary," I remarked.

"Perhaps," she said, still looking at me. "He is a strange man, Mr. Thiel. Not an easy man."

"You approve of him?

"Yes. But we are two of a kind."

"I cannot imagine disliking someone of whom you approve, Aunt." That was true. "I wouldn't need to see very much of him, would I?"

"Perhaps not." She thought for a minute. "You are considering this position."

"Yes. Unless you think I shouldn't."

"There is so much you do not know. Let me tell you what I can. Then you can think carefully about it, and we will write to Mr. Thiel tomorrow."

I waited while she collected her thoughts. It seemed to be hard for her. Finally, she said, "Let's ask Martha to bring us a pot of tea and sit in the visitors' chairs."

Aunt Constance's office had two parts to it. One was the

desk area, with bookshelves and two extra, straight-backed chairs. This was by the long windows and during the daytime was filled with light. When Aunt Constance sat there she was businesslike and serious, quick and sharp in her words. The other part of the room, the visitors' section, consisted of two chairs and a small sofa near the fireplace. The chairs were softer and upholstered with a rich fabric embroidered with exotic birds and foliage. Here, parents and visitors talked about the school with my aunt, and tea was served them on small tables. Here was where conversations took place about a student's progress, or Aunt Constance's educational beliefs. Here there were places where shadows softened the bright clear light of day.

Martha brought in a tray of tea and placed it before Aunt Constance. Silently, Aunt Constance poured my cup, adding sugar and milk generously. She took her own tea with just a slice of lemon. All the time, I knew, her mind was working, and I watched her face, trying to understand what she might be thinking.

"Perhaps," I suggested, "Miss Worthy would be a better candidate. She is not a child, but surely she is too old for impropriety."

Aunt Constance laughed. "You do not know Marlborough. You have been raised too near the city to understand country villages, especially country villages with only one important family. You and I know how safe Miss Worthy would be. But the townspeople have rich imaginations and little to exercise them on."

"How could people be so foolish?"

"People can be unimaginably foolish," Aunt Constance said, and then added quietly, "and they can be unimaginably grand, at times." This was the kind of statement she would never make in the clear light, or over the flat surface of her desk.

"Marlborough is a small village, in the Berkshire

Mountains. Most of the few inhabitants are farmers, or practice a trade connected with farming. Some twenty years ago, a wealthy man named Josiah Callender decided to retire there. His reasons for this were, I think, admirable ones. He purchased a large tract of land and rented out most of it to local farmers, on generous terms. The main house he occupied himself, with his daughter Irene. Nearby he built a second large house for his son Enoch and Enoch's new bride. The Callenders lived there, live there still I suppose, much as the great lords once lived in Europe.

"I knew Irene Callender, which is how I come to know this. We had been girls together in New York State. Irene was always most enthusiastic about my beliefs, and it was greatly due to her help that this school got started. Irene was a dear friend, a good friend."

Something in Aunt Constance's voice told me that this friend was now dead.

"Irene had rather a hard life. Although the family was wealthy, it was plagued by ill luck. Her mother died giving birth to Enoch, so Irene had the primary responsibility for raising the boy, who was six years younger than she. She was a large girl, not pretty in the accepted sense, dark, with strong features, unflirtatious, without any vanity. More than this, she mistrusted the few men who courted her, suspecting that they were after her money. I believe she was correct in her suspicion.

"She devoted her life to her brother and to her father. When they moved to Marlborough, she was confirmed an old maid. On the whole, she was contented with that.

"In Marlborough, she met Daniel Thiel and married him."

"Mr. Thiel?" I was surprised. "Why?"

"She loved him. She admired his paintings. She approved of his actions during the War Between the States."

"What did he do?"

"It was what he did not do: he refused to go to war. Like our Mr. Thoreau. Only Mr. Thiel did not have the advantages of good birth and important friends. He was the son of a farmer, a man who owned his own land but could not afford to educate his sons, or to purchase replacements who would enter the army in their steads. So that when he was conscripted, Mr. Thiel fled to the mountains and lived there alone."

"He was one of the Hiders," I cried. I had been taught that these were ignoble people. Both of Aunt Constance's brothers had died in the War Between the States, one at Gettysburg, one in a prison hospital in Atlanta. Her father had broken his health when he went down to the notorious Andersonville prison to be a minister to the prisoners, and died soon thereafter. "Why is he your friend?"

Aunt Constance smiled. "It is an often-difficult friendship, but I do trust him. At the time, his family felt he had disgraced them. They moved away from the area. The farm was sold. After the war Mr. Thiel returned to Marlborough, although the villagers avoided him. I don't believe that bothered him. He married Irene. They lived together in the big house quite happily, I believe, for four years. Then he lost her, and at the same time their child. There was talk, of course; in such places as Marlborough there is always talk. He became once again a recluse, living in that same house with only a housekeeper, and she a woman who had been in prison." Aunt Constance reached out to refill her teacup.

"I suspect that the only time Mr. Thiel meets people is when he comes to Boston, to put his pictures into the hands of a dealer and to dine with us."

"No wonder he is such an awkward guest," I said.

"No wonder."

"Mrs. Bywall is the housekeeper?" I asked. "Why was she sent to prison?"

"She had stolen something—spoons or a brooch, some-

8

thing of that sort—from the house where she was employed as a maid. It came out that she had a brother who was mortally ill and needed medicines, which the family could not afford. But still, she had stolen. So she was sent to prison for ten years."

"How did Mr. Thiel become involved with her?"

"The house in which she was employed was that of his brother-in-law, Enoch Callender."

I sat quietly and thought, carefully. "It sounds a most unfortunate household into which I am invited."

"Yes," Aunt Constance said. "Certainly not an easy one to work in."

"Yet you believe I could do it."

"I believe you could do the work," she said. "It is the people who trouble me."

Chapter Two

With Aunt Constance's consent and, I thought, approval, I decided to go. I knew immediately that I would do so, but I followed Aunt Constance's advice and thought about it. Or, rather, I tried to think about it because I knew Aunt Constance believed I would do so. She had taught me to think carefully, but I do not know if she did so because she guessed how hasty and willful my nature was. I always tried to comply with her wishes. Orphaned herself at a young age, raised by distant relatives and possessed of only a small inheritance with which to support and educate herself, Aunt Constance had a strength I could only wish to emulate. Her early sorrows had given her a sympathetic heart and a rare quality of wisdom. So that night I sat at my desk trying to consider the offer Mr. Thiel had made. But I must admit that the chance to try my hand at real work—to earn a sum that might be put aside to defray the cost of my education—

occupied more of my thoughts than it should have. The worst of it would be, I thought, the solitude. Yet, accustomed as I was to Aunt Constance's company, I still believed that I could keep my own company tolerably well.

It was agreed that I would work for Mr. Thiel during the months of July and August. Mr. Thiel offered me forty dollars, to be paid at the end of the summer, less whatever small sums I might need during the time.

Aunt Constance called in her dressmaker. We ordered two light and simple blue dresses, with plain white collars and cuffs, made of sturdy gabardine. The dresses arrived shortly before I was to leave. There was a surprise in the box with the plain dresses: a lightweight, delicate dress, rosy pink with little flowers printed all over it. I was speechless.

"You like it," Aunt Constance observed, with one of her warm smiles.

"Very much," I told her truthfully. "Thank you. But why?"

"You may need it. You may not, after all; but if you do need such a dress I thought this fabric would do admirably. Also, because I shall miss you. We have never been parted for long."

I understood her. I had, naturally, had more misgivings about the employment, the closer the actual day of departure came. It often happens that way. When a daring idea first crosses one's mind, if it is to be realized in the future it is often appealing. Then, as the time for its execution comes nearer, one begins to dread that which had once been anticipated. I told myself this was mere human nature. However, I was finding human nature a little uncomfortable, easier to name than to overcome. At our last breakfast I was afraid I might cry. I had trouble eating my egg and toast with my usual appetite.

"You will write to me?" Aunt Constance asked. Like me, she was eating little. "I will be interested to hear how the work goes. And I admit to a certain curiosity about your responses to these people. It has been many years since I visited the Berkshires. Many years. It is very beautiful country. Do you remember the name of the station at which you are to debark?"

"North Adams," I said. "Mr. Thiel will meet me. If for any reason he cannot be there I am to go to the Grand Chisholm Hotel, where they will expect me. The hotel is directly across the street from the railway station."

"You do understand that Mr. Thiel and I will be sympathetic if, for any reason, you want to return home before the time is up," Aunt Constance said.

I nodded. And I held my tongue.

"You are young," Aunt Constance said. "I begin to wonder if we are wise to do this."

I sounded as cheerful as I could: "We can but try. How often have you told me that women must learn that they are as brave as men?"

"Men can be foolhardy."

"Well, we will not fall into that trap, will we? I am not helpless, you know."

She laughed. "To think that you are comforting me. No, you are not helpless. You are strong, healthy, able to amuse yourself, and you have a bold mind. Forgive me, my dear, for the megrims. Men, and women too, are unpredictable creatures. You have seen little of this. I wonder now if your innocence is enough protection for you."

Aunt Constance accompanied me into Boston and helped me find a seat in the railway coach on the Boston and Maine Railroad. My one portmanteau and the basket that held my lunch were placed on the seat next to me.

"I shall think of you," I told Aunt Constance.

"You will do well," she assured me.

Despite the grime of the locomotive and the steam rising along its sides, I leaned out the window and looked back to her, waving, until she had dwindled out of sight. Then I sat back, to attempt to think cheerfully. The journey, more than a hundred miles, was longer than any I had ever taken, and I hoped I would enjoy it. I determined to forget about my destination and what awaited me there.

The train made its noisy way through the outskirts of Boston, then through farmlands much like those I had always known. Gradually, the towns grew farther apart. In the early afternoon, the landscape became hilly. Trees were in full foliage. The rivers we crossed, the lakes we chugged beside, sparkled in sunlight. Often farmer's children would stand at the side of the tracks to watch the train go by, their eyes staring into the coaches.

We arrived at North Adams as the sun set. Twilight shadows made the air chilly. I disembarked with as much confidence as I could muster. I had reason not to be concerned, should Mr. Thiel not be there. I knew what I was to do—I would cross over to the hotel and sleep the night there. Were he not to come at all, I would merely return to Cambridge the next day.

No such difficulty faced me. He stood waiting in a shadow, a wide hat hiding his eyes. He let me stand before him for a moment before he reached down to take my portmanteau.

"So. You came," he said. He was taller than I had remembered.

"Yes," I said. I could think of nothing else to say.

"I thought you might change your mind at the last minute."

"As you can see, sir, I did not, for here I am."

"Yes," he agreed. We stood thus a long moment. "I have in mind to go straight to Marlborough." He did not ask me if I were too tired for a journey of several hours nor if I would prefer to rest the night at the hotel before going on.

"I can make the journey," I said. He turned and led the

way to an open carriage that stood before the station. He placed my portmanteau in it, helped me into a seat and then climbed up to the driver's seat.

Then he turned around and spoke to me out of the darkness. "Have you dined?"

"No, sir," I said.

"You should have spoken up," he grumbled.

We ate at the hotel; or, more truthfully, I ate and he watched me. He had, he told me, eaten while waiting for the train. It is not easy to eat while you are being closely watched by a silent and impatient stranger. I felt awkward and hurried. I declined the dessert I wanted for the sake of his impatience.

"You shouldn't do that," he remarked as we walked back to the carriage along the dark and silent street.

"Do what?"

"Go without something you want for somebody else's convenience."

"I'm sorry," I apologized without thinking. Then I grew angry. "It was obvious that you were eager to be on your way," I pointed out to him.

"I am, of course," he said. "But that should make no difference to you. Your Aunt Constance wouldn't have done it."

"Perhaps not," I agreed. "However, she might have. If it had been she, she would have contrived it so cleverly that you would not have noticed it."

"True," he agreed. He said no more to me.

At the start of that dark ride, I could see only the back of the man as he kept the horses to a comfortable trot. In the darkness he could have been anyone, taking me anywhere, the devil himself, hurrying me to some dismal destination. He made no sound, neither talked nor whistled. I, too, said nothing. I felt oddly helpless, a feeling new to me. Fortunately, I also felt a little angry still, and it was this that kept back the tears so near the surface. What, after all, was I doing here, with this unfriendly and forbidding man? As my eyes grew accustomed, I could pick out the shapes of trees passing along beside us, growing thick overhead, and even the back of the horse steadily pulling the carriage down the dark road. The sound of the horse's hooves on the packed road was steady, monotonous. At last, exhausted by the long day, I fell asleep.

If you have ever awakened in a room that was not familiar, you can imagine how I felt. For a moment, looking around the plain room, with its one window facing east (the sun on my face had woken me), its whitewashed walls, its narrow dresser, its one chair and writing table beside the empty stone fireplace, I was sure I was still asleep and that when the dream was finished I would find myself in my own accustomed room. I closed my eyes to await that second awakening and only then noticed that I was still fully clothed, except for my shoes. I began to remember where I might be. Someone—Mr. Thiel himself—must have carried me in and put me to bed.

It is a fearful thing to realize you are alone in a strange place, among strangers.

I got out of bed and went to the window. I could see a red barn, with a carriage standing before it. Beyond that, to one side, was another, smaller outbuilding. What was probably a vegetable garden was also visible. My bedroom must be at the back of the house, I thought. All around, as far as I could tell, were trees, and hills tall enough to be called mountains.

While I unpacked my suitcase, changed into fresh clothes, and washed my face and hands at the basin on the dresser, I considered what to do next. I opened the door and listened. I could hear nothing.

The hallway was narrow and only dimly lit. It seemed to

lead toward the front of the house. I passed a few closed doors and came to an intersection of hall and stairs. There, a tall window looked out over the lawns and driveway to more forest and hills. The house seemed to be set at the top of one of the smaller hills. I could see the green commons and some rooftops of a town, set some distance below the house. There should, I remembered, be at least one other house quite near here, the house Josiah Callender had built for his son. There was no sign of it. I descended the staircase.

All the floors were deeply polished wood, and the stair boards creaked under my feet. I hoped somebody would hear me and come forward, but nobody did. On the main floor I looked through large open double doors to the dining room and saw that the long table had one place set at it. I would have preferred to go out onto the porch, which stretched along the front of the house and thence onto the lawn, but I decided it was necessary to first find whoever was in the house. So I crossed the dining room to enter what I thought must be the kitchen.

There I saw a woman sitting at a table drinking from a cup and reading a periodical. She was engrossed in her reading. Her arms, with the sleeves of her dress rolled up, showed heavy. Her face was round and pale. She wore an apron. Her colorless hair was simply done, pulled back to the top of her head, to be out of her way, I thought. Her face was expressionless as she read, her lips moved forming the words silently.

"Excuse me," I said. She started and looked up at me. She struggled clumsily to her feet.

"You must be Mrs. Bywall," I said, walking up to her and holding out my hand. She wiped hers on her stained apron and shook mine firmly. Mrs. Bywall was a short, stout body. She looked both hardy and strong.

"I am Jean Wainwright," I said.

"I know that. I was listening for you. But I didn't hear you. You're a quiet thing."

"I hope I didn't frighten you."

"It would take more than a child to do that," she said. Then she closed her pale lips over whatever else she might have wanted to say and waited, considering me, for a long moment before she spoke again. When she did, the words came hastily stumbling out. "You must be hungry. Mr. Thiel said I wasn't to waken you. I said as how it might be easier on you, in this strange place, to breakfast with him, but he said no, you were to sleep. I don't argue with him. Now he's gone off to his studio and won't be in until lunch. He's not to be interrupted when he's working." Again she paused, again resumed speech: "He said you were to eat and then to walk about the place. What will you like for your breakfast? Mr. Thiel said I was to sit with you." The pale lips closed. There was no expression on her face or in her eyes as she spoke, as if she were a child rehearsing a set piece.

I was bewildered. I waited to see if she would stumble into speech again. I didn't know what I was supposed to say.

"What will you have for breakfast, Miss Wainwright?"

"Must you call me that?" I asked.

"Miss Jean then. What will you have, Miss Jean? Egg, sausage, porridge, cocoa, rolls, milk, wheatcakes? I don't know what they serve in the city for breakfast. Mr. Thiel never tells me such things." The lips closed again.

"Ordinarily I have an egg and toast, with a glass of milk. Would that be all right?"

"Of course it will be all right." She turned abruptly from me and went into a pantry at the back of the kitchen. I had a minute to look around at the large low-ceilinged room. It was a room with a warm feeling to it, with bright yellow wooden cupboards and scoured wooden countertops. Sunlight poured into it, and the door to the back was opened onto a small porch, showing also the barn and garden.

When Mrs. Bywall returned, carrying eggs and a loaf of bread as well as a pitcher, I stood where I had.

"You just go sit down and wait then. It won't take but a minute," Mrs. Bywall told me, without a smile, turning to the old-fashioned wood stove.

She served the meal on plain stoneware. There was much more food than I was accustomed to. Mrs. Bywall had scrambled several eggs and brought me a basket of sliced bread, three kinds of jam, and a bowl of butter. Milk was poured from the pitcher, and the pitcher left on the table. Mrs. Bywall sat down opposite me, heavily. She watched me eat. I tried to pay no attention.

"It's too much," I apologized when I had eaten as much as I could.

"I'll learn your appetite," she said. "I'm not sure what girls eat, so I tried to remember what my brothers ate at your age. They were always hungry. But then, I don't imagine you've ever gone short of food, so perhaps it's different."

"It is all delicious," I said. It was, fresh and light, the eggs hot, the milk cool.

Mrs. Bywall looked at me sharply and began to speak, apparently a painful task. "I've been in jail," she announced abruptly. Her eyes were on her hands, clasped together on the tabletop. "I spent ten years in there. There are people would say I'm not fit company for a child. Not Mr. Thiel, not him, but you might think that yourself—" I wanted to answer her then but her voice went on, as if the words had been memorized. "You should know that, Mr. Thiel says. I was sixteen at the time, and my brother was sick, a lung infection, my brother Horace. He needed medicines and a long stay at a spa in Virginia. My parents were tenant farmers. The farm was small and there had been two bad years. My husband—newly wed I was, to Charlie Bywall, also a farming man—he had nothing to help us with. I went to work at the other house," she pointed with her chin, down the hill. "And I stole six silver spoons. Sterling silver, they were, from London. I knew it was wrong. But Horace coughed all night. We had to have the money. It was old Dr. Carter, who would give farmers no credit, nor charity.

"Mr. Callender prosecuted—Mr. Enoch that is. And I went to jail." She looked at me then, without really seeing me. "They are terrible places, cruel, unclean. I don't think of that. It was a long time, ten years. . . . My husband, my Charlie, he left. I never heard from him again. Horace died. My father came to see me, once or twice, but it was too cruel so I asked him to stay away. When I came out—people stayed away from me. I thought of leaving the village. My family. But where would I go? Until Mr. Thiel hired me here. He had had his troubles too, I learned, although I wasn't here during those years. He knows what it is like. He knows what it is to have people stare at you and talk about you and pretend you aren't there. There was his wife, first, and then the child—and I never believed what people said about either of them." At this point she stopped, and looked at me, just a brief glance. She waited before beginning again. "Mr. Thiel asked me to come and keep house here, so I did. Of course I did. Where else could I have gotten work? So now you know what I am."

"I knew you had been in jail," I said. "My Aunt Constance told me before. She didn't think it was important, that you had been—" I couldn't say the word again.

"Then she must be an unusual woman. Sending you here, too, to him."

With her story told, Mrs. Bywall became almost at ease.

I could understand how hard it must have been for her to tell that to an unknown girl. She told me what time luncheon would be served and advised me to go about outside, instructing me what I would and would not want to see. "You won't want to walk down to the village your first day. They'll know you're here, of course, they always know everything. I can't think they'll be so cruel to a child— although come to think of it, you're not so much younger than I was when my troubles came. But you won't want to go there yet." Between each piece of advice she hesitated, as if to be sure not to give anything away. "And you mustn't go near Mr. Thiel's studio. He'd fair frighten you back to Boston if you did that. That's the small building, beyond the barn, with the great glass windows. A glazier from Albany put those in, but that was when Mr. Thiel's wife was alive and her father. They spent money, those Callenders. Mr. Callender—" she stopped. I waited. "Mr. Thiel said I wasn't to talk your ears off," she said uneasily. "He said you were a silent little creature—and that you certainly are. Can you do this work?"

I smiled. "I don't know. My aunt thinks I can, and so apparently does Mr. Thiel."

Mrs. Bywall did not answer my smile.

"Imagine being so educated and still so young. I did learn how to read in jail, there was that. A spinster woman came to teach us, all Bible and sin, some minister's daughter I don't doubt. But I did learn that."

There were questions I wanted to ask Mrs. Bywall, which I did not dare to voice. What she said, the words she spoke, were not unfriendly; but her face never showed any expression, as if—she were afraid of what she might say, or of somebody who was listening to everything she said, somebody who had told her what to say and what not to say. So I merely thanked her and excused myself from the table.

I spent the rest of the morning exploring. First I looked briefly at the downstairs rooms. The house seemed old, plain but comfortable. A large library, opposite to the dining room, took up most of the ground floor. Books lined the walls, and the floor had two faded oriental rugs on it. Besides the usual fireplace and chairs for reading, there was a huge desk, a long table and a grand piano.

Next to the dining room I found a small parlor, never used by the looks of it. Its chairs and table, lamps and windows, were shrouded with sheets. The air smelled musty. By then I wanted only to go outside. The house was too dark, too silent. I felt as though I were an intruder, out of place. I feared to go somewhere I shouldn't. So I ignored the last closed door and went back down the hall to the open front door.

Outside, the sky shone blue and the sun shone warm. Trees and mountains surrounded the house, protectively it seemed. I turned back from the driveway to look at the place where I was to live for the next months, if all went well. The main house, with the long kitchen wing, like a capital *P* laid on its back, was entirely built of gray stone. The roof was made of slate shingles. Two tall stone chimneys marked the ends of the main house, while a smaller chimney emerged from the kitchen wing. It was simple, plain and rather handsome.

I wandered down the driveway, a dirt road leading away from the house. Soon trees closed over my head, their full foliage providing cool shade. Beyond the bird and insect noises, I heard water running. I turned off the road to the right and found a small river. Near the banks the water was shallow and clear, merry indeed, as it passed quickly over stones, running down the steep hill. I took off my shoes and stockings to wade in it. The mud bottom oozed between my toes, the water ran around my ankles, and it was altogether delightful. I kept carefully back from the deep center as I followed the bank down, listening to the brief songs of birds overhead, and a faint rustle of leaves at the tops of the overgrowing trees. I held my skirts high so that the water that played around my ankles would not dampen them. The cool water felt delicious. It is not surprising that I followed the river too far. I almost walked into view of the green lawn of another house, built of gray stone like Mr. Thiel's.

I was stopped from actually walking into view by the sound of voices. I stepped back into the protecting trees on the bank. For a short time (just until my conscience got the better of me) I spied on a group of people who were out on that green lawn.

A woman sat under a tree in one of three lawn chairs with a tall glass on the table beside her and a parasol held open to protect her face from the sun. Two boys, one almost a man, it seemed, played at croquet with a young lady. All of these people were finely dressed, the boys in crisp white suits and the ladies in white gowns. The only conversation that drifted down to my ears had to do with quarrels about the rules of the game. Then a man wearing a white suit emerged from the house. All conversation stopped.

He was a handsome figure, with golden hair and a bold, free stride as he crossed the lawn. Tall, graceful, a golden man—he was unlike any man I had seen before. The men I had seen wore somber clothing and moved as if they were always thinking of their dignity. This man broke into a run as he hurried to join the young people at croquet. He picked up a mallet and whirled it around over his head, turning in circles but never the least off balance. The young people gathered up their balls to start a new game. One by one, he let them start before him, the youngest first. He bowed and gestured with an arm to each in turn. When his own turn came he went easily to place the ball then planted his feet as carefully and precisely as a circus acrobat before making his play.

When I finally turned away from the picture of the green lawn and made my way back up through the cool waters, I thought that this house, so like Mr. Thiel's, must be the home of the Callenders, so that the man must be Enoch Callender, the woman his wife, and the three young people his children. I did not, beyond that, think any more of them because I just then realized I was in danger of being late for luncheon.

Chapter Three

I was not late but I had no time to tidy myself before sitting
down to table other than to slip into the kitchen to wash my
hands. Aunt Constance would have sent me upstairs, but
Mr. Thiel did not seem to notice my disarranged hair and
heated face.

I was seated where I had eaten breakfast, and Mr. Thiel
sat where Mrs. Bywall had, across from me, but only the
width across. This became our habitual way of eating
together. The food was simple and good. I was, I discovered, quite hungry. For a while we ate silently, then he
started a conversation.

"Mrs. Bywall spoke with you?"

"Yes," I said.

"Do you wish to leave?"

"No," I said.

He returned to his food. When he had cleaned his plate,

he sat looking at me, waiting for me to finish. I found his stare most uncomfortable. Mr. Thiel was a straight man, he carried himself straight, his short, graying hair was straight, his glance was cold and straight. He had a hard face, filled with character, I supposed, but not attractive and not welcoming. There are, I think, two sorts of faces that people have. The first is welcoming and responds visibly to what it sees. The other is secretive, or private. It is closed off and seems to protect itself from whatever it is facing. Mr. Thiel had this second kind of face. The difference is, I think, in the eyes themselves. Eyes hold the essential expression of a face. A man can smile with his mouth, but his eyes will give away his real thoughts. Aunt Constance had a stern expression, but her eyes were always welcoming. Mr. Thiel had a way of looking through his eyes as if through a microscope at some strange, and possibly distasteful, creature.

When I had finished my meal—which I obstinately ate at my own pace—I put down my own knife and fork carefully, as I had been taught, at twenty past two. "Aunt Constance had already spoken to me of Mrs. Bywall," I informed him.

"I thought she might."

Even though I could see that he was not interested in my reaction, I told him what I felt.

"It is a sad story."

He shrugged.

"Mrs. Bywall seems very loyal to you."

"She has reason to be, although it's no credit to me. People are such fools," he said.

"Not all," I protested.

"Those who aren't are so few they make no difference."

I couldn't agree with him but couldn't argue. So I sat silent as Mrs. Bywall brough in a hot cherry pie.

"Are you ready to begin your work now?" Mr. Thiel

asked me, as if it had been days, not merely a morning, since I had arrived, as if I had been shirking.

"Of course," I said. "But just what is it you want me to do?" The question seemed to annoy him.

"My late father-in-law, Josiah Callender, left several boxes of papers. Letters, essays, I don't know what, stored up in the attic. You are to sort through them, separate the wheat from the chaff, and determine what should be done with the papers."

I looked up in surprise. "How can I decide that?"

"That's up to you. I suppose you can, or you wouldn't be here. I don't expect to be bothered with the task, in any way." He ate his pie methodically.

"But how can I know what is important?" I insisted.

He sighed, and answered me. "Given a choice between a formal and meaningless note from President Lincoln, say, and a letter to Josiah Callender from his father, instructing him in the duites of married life, which would you keep?"

I thought carefully about this. "I would keep both," I decided. "The one might be of monetary value, or value to the family for the pride of it, if it were signed by Mr. Lincoln himself. The other would certainly be of historical value."

He said nothing. He just nodded his head.

"Do you know anything about the Callenders?" he asked after a time.

"Almost nothing."

"I suppose you should know something. Josiah's father made a fortune in munitions during the War Between the States. Not a great fortune, but a substantial one. Josiah, however, was a man of conscience. He couldn't rest easy with money made from blood, as he understood it. However, he was not a man of courage. It wasn't until his father died, in the seventies, that Josiah made his stand against the old man. At that time, Josiah sold the factories and moved here, bringing his family with him. His wife had died, many years earlier, giving birth to the second child, a boy. The boy was raised by his sister, who was some six years older than he. I say nothing about Enoch. The sister, Irene, was my wife for a short time."

"She was Aunt Constance's friend."

I thought he might say more about his wife's character, but he didn't.

"Irene had promised her father that she would see that the family papers were properly attended to, but she died unexpectedly, shortly after Josiah. I consider myself bound by my wife's promise. I do not expect that you will find much of value or much to be preserved. Josiah Callender was rare enough, an honest man with the intent to do good: but such men are not important."

"Perhaps not," I said in such a way that he had to hear in my voice how little I agreed with him. For some reason I was offended at his dismissal of his father-in-law. "Certainly they are at least admirable."

Mr. Thiel said nothing, but his mouth curved in a smile. It was not a smile that reached to his eyes, not a comfortable, pleasant smile, and I felt that I had been silly. I was not going to enjoy his company. Neither would he enjoy mine, he had made that clear already. But I was there to do a job, and I supposed we would manage to see very little of one another, which seemed the best possible state of affairs.

I followed Mr. Thiel into the library. There, lined up on the floor, were a dozen wooden crates, each painted with a large Roman numeral, each with the top partially lifted. Except for the twelfth, which I noticed was only half full. It had no top. It looked as if papers had been dumped into it, higglety-pigglety. The twelve boxes took up a great deal of floor space.

"Are all the boxes like that?" I asked, indicating the half-full one.

"Nobody said it would be easy. My wife and her father accumulated papers in their desks. Two or three times a year, they would empty the desk drawers into these boxes. When a box was full, a top would be nailed on it."

"Oh." I hadn't realized there would be so much. I was dismayed by the size of the task.

"You're supposed to know what to do," Mr. Thiel reminded me.

"I think I had better read through some of the first box and then I will know better." I didn't want him to see how overwhelmed I felt. Aunt Constance couldn't have guessed at the size of the task, or she wouldn't have advised me to accept the job. But I wouldn't have him think I was discomfited.

"I'm not going to worry about it at all, Jean. That is your job. You may use this room as your own. The table is clear. I have no idea what may be in the desk. My own sitting room is across the hall."

"I thought so," I said, thinking of the closed door.

He looked at me coldly.

"I was told to look about this morning," I reminded him. "I didn't look in there, but I did look in the others."

"Ordinarily I work at the studio during the morning and am out during the afternoons. I expect you should have some time for whatever childish amusements are necessary for good health, so you might follow the same schedule."

I agreed.

"We do not attend church, but there is no reason why you shouldn't."

"Thank you. I will think of it."

He waited. I waited for him to leave. Finally I said, "I will begin this afternoon, just to get started. If that is agreeable to you."

He turned to go without a word.

"How did the boxes get in here?" I asked his back. "They weren't here this morning."

"I brought them down. We waited luncheon for you." He left. Mr. Thiel seemed to like having the last word. While I was still forming an apology, I was left alone with these dozen boxes, each as large as a trunk. For a time, I looked about the room, then out the windows, while my mind worked at the problem. Of course, I needed to read whatever was in there, and apparently from the bottom of the box up, which seemed a needless complication. I went to the desk and started pulling out the drawers. Some kind of sorting of the papers would be neccessary. The desk drawers were empty, but not large enough to be useful in that task. The center drawer, unlike the six side drawers, was locked. I wondered why, naturally, but thought no more about it.

Instead, I began box *1*. I pulled off the top completely, took an armload of papers and envelopes and carried them to the table. Working methodically, from left to right, I covered the table. When the bottom layer was clear I took that in a pile to the desk, where I sat to read. Before I concentrated on the task before me, a question formed itself in my mind: Why had Aunt Constance said that she and Mr. Thiel were two of a kind? As far as I could tell, they were two different kinds; the one kind, humorous, warm; the other selfish and perhaps cold-hearted.

I began the Callender Papers. The library was a good room for such work—cool, even in the heat of the day, and quiet. A proper room for slow, careful work.

During the next days I became accustomed to the task and the house and, to an extent, to my companions, both the living and the dead. I found that I could sort the early papers out into groups, personal and family papers, public papers, business-of-life papers (Josiah married young, at twenty, just after leaving Harvard; his wife was extravagant, or so I concluded from dressmaker, milliner and jeweler bills). The papers included his letters to the girl he married, which she had saved, and hers to him. She had kept his letters tied together into a neat bundle, which she then wrapped in a piece of yellow silk. Those he had received from her were scattered through the bottom of the box. More interesting were some letters to the young Josiah from his father, which indicated the character of his father: an energetic man, who had made his fortune by a combination of shrewdness, luck and—if Josiah's description of the purchase of the munitions factory in 1851 was accurate—a certain disregard of the fine points of the laws of both God and men. The father seemed to scorn his son's character and opinions, condemning him as impractical, idealistic and ungrateful. They lived apart and corresponded infrequently. Josiah wrote dutifully once every month, and his father almost never. I found myself unexpectedly interested in these people, filled with curiosity about what they were like, what would happen to them. I found myself taking pleasure in those quiet hours in the library.

While I learned more of the family history during the mornings, I used the afternoons to learn more about the countryside. I did not walk down along the river again, toward the other house. Instead, I walked upriver, uphill. I grew more at ease in the forests, more adept at crossing the uneven landscapes. I began to recognize the different creatures and the sounds they made. Moreover, the cool of the silent trees, the running of the water, the occasional open glade, all gave me pleasure. I was glad to be alone there, to think my own thoughts. Once away from Mr. Thiel's house, I saw no human creature, and I quickly recognized the particular pleasures of rural solitude, so different from everything I had known before. Nobody disturbed my afternoons in the woods.

On one of the first of those afternoons I discovered a small waterfall a half-mile north of the house and it became a place I often returned to. (When I first saw it, it seemed to welcome me.) At that point in its course, the river ran down through a sharp ravine. The ravine was no more than twelve feet deep, but its sides were steep and rocky. The water cascaded over a small falls, perhaps six feet high, into a dark pool. It hesitated there a minute before rushing on over the shallower, wider bed below. On the bluff above this pool, two old beech trees gave shade and offered roots to sit upon. Across the way, dense forest grew up around the great gray boulders. The place was filled with the sound of the water. It filled me with peace, a sense of familiarity and security.

I often needed that sense of peace and security. I found Mr. Thiel an uncomfortable man to live with. He was silent most of the time and made me feel an intruder. I told myself that he would have treated whoever came to do this job as little more than an inconvenience. He was acceding to his late wife's wishes, not seeking company. Company was the last thing he wanted, that he made clear; he made no effort to win my friendship. Rather, he seemed bent upon appearing at his worst, or so it seemed—truculent and unwelcoming. When he spoke at all, he spoke brusquely. Not from anger, although he often made me angry, but from impatience. Mrs. Bywall, on the other hand, would suddenly burst into speech on some trivial subject and then just as suddenly clamp her lips shut to relapse into uneasy silence. Both of them seemed to find life unpleasant. With neither of these personalities could I be at ease. To make it worse, both thought little of their fellow creatures. Both expected the worst. We never know what will happen to us, of course, and I know I cannot now say that I will never come to share such an opinion of the world, but I did not share the opinion then and I could not agree with them. I was not, however, encouraged to speak my own mind on the subject. I was expected, apparently, merely to listen. This was difficult because Aunt Constance had not raised me to be seen but not heard, like so many children. I chafed under the treatment.

Several days after I had arrived at his house, Mr. Thiel announced at luncheon that he and I would walk down to the village. "It is nearly three miles," he added. "You will need good walking shoes and a shawl."

His assumption that I could not think that out for myself irritated me. "I know," I said. I had already noted that, despite the warmth of the days, the evenings came early and cool to the mountains. Mr. Thiel heard the irritation in my voice and raised his eyebrows. The gesture might have meant anything, even disapproval: I could not tell. I did not much care.

So we walked together, following the dirt road that followed the brook. Mr. Thiel knew a great deal about the trees, birds and undergrowth. For some reason, he instructed me about them as we walked. Although his superior tone was irritating to me, I was eager to learn how to differentiate these and discover what their properties were. As we walked, I listened carefully and tried to remember. I wanted him to see, too, that I could learn rapidly. I hoped, I think, that he might learn to respect my intelligence at least.

We passed the other house, barely visible at the back of its broad lawn. "Is that where Mr. Enoch Callender lives?" I asked.

"Yes."

"What does he look like?" I asked.

"Look like? Like a Greek statue come to life," Mr. Thiel said. Then it was the man I saw.

"You don't maintain ties with him?" I asked. It was an impertinent question.

"No," Mr. Thiel said, briefly. "Have you met him in your wanderings?"

"No. Do you forbid it?"

"Forbid you to meet him? Them? He has a family. Why should you want to meet them?"

I answered as directly as he questioned: "I don't *want* to meet them. But if I should, in my wanderings as you say, meet him, I wonder what you ask of me."

"I ask nothing," he said. "There's little danger of meeting, unless you trespass. They seldom go off the lawns."

My curiosity was aroused. What had happened here? The two houses did not communicate, that was obvious. Mr. Thiel did not like the Callenders; that too was obvious. Why should he refer to the danger of such a meeting, except to put me on my guard, or prejudice me against the inhabitants of the house? Did he fear them? Then why did he remain on the Callender property? What held him in Marlborough?

Chapter Four

The village of Marlborough lies in a small, oval valley. Hills rise all around it. The river, widened and deepened, runs the length of the valley.

The road from Mr. Thiel's home joined the one village street just before a stone bridge arched over the river. There, we stopped.

"I am going to the bank and to the store," he said, indicating two solitary brick buildings off to the left. A row of white clapboard houses faced these buildings, each house set in its own generous lawn. "Is there any purchase you would like to make?"

"No," I said.

"No letter to mail?"

"No."

"I have written your aunt to report your safe arrival," he said.

"I have been waiting to write until I feel settled," I told him. "That was what Aunt Constance requested me to do." Who was he to remind me to write to my aunt?

He bowed his head to me, formally. "Do you feel settled?"

For some reason, I could not lie to him, not even for the sake of politeness. Neither, for the sake of politeness, could I tell him the precise truth. "More so than at first. I feel settled enough to write, of course."

"I am flattered to hear it." He did not sound flattered. "Perhaps then you might like to visit our church, which lies over the bridge."

I agreed to that and we parted. We made no plans for meeting again. His discourtesy neither surprised nor dismayed me. I could certainly make my way back to the house on my own, and I assumed it was his intention that I do so. His displeasure in my company didn't concern me, except to raise the question of why he had bothered to summon me there at all. The papers had rested ignored for years, there was no urgency to sort and catalogue them. I wondered if he had some other purpose for me—what it might be I could not guess. He was a man who kept his own counsel. I crossed the bridge, heading toward the steeple visible nearby through treetops. A boy was fishing off the bank on the far side of the bridge. I ignored him, as he did me.

The church was a square, forbidding building. The big wooden doors were open, but I was not tempted inside. It was too dark, too empty. Instead, I walked behind it to a graveyard.

A graveyard can be a pleasant place. I do not believe in ghosts, so there is nothing to fear from the dead. The tombstones tell of other lives, now ended. It doesn't matter that some are poor and some rich, that some graves are marked by simple crosses while others have marble statuary. Such equality seems a useful lesson to learn, in this world.

The Marlborough graveyard was small, modest compared to St. Auburn Cemetery near Boston. But it was beautiful, with tall oak trees and delicate dogwoods scattered among the stones. The mountains seemed somehow to be guarding it. I thought to myself as I walked through it that it would be a good place to lie for all of time. The Callender area was separated from the rest of the cemetery by a wrought iron fence, but the gate was open so I went in. Only two graves occupied the large area, leaving room for many more. Both tombstones were unadorned marble, both apparently cut by the same craftsman. Josiah Callender had died on May 9, 1884; his daughter Irene on May 15 of the same year. Beneath the name Irene Callender Thiel was inscribed the message, "beloved wife of Daniel Thiel, beloved mother."

I returned to the village, walking slowly, thinking of the letter I would write to Aunt Constance that evening, wondering where old Enoch Callender was buried. As I approached the bridge, I saw that the boy was still there. His birch rod arced over the water, and he was standing. I had arrived just as he was about to catch a fish. I stayed to watch. I'd never seen a fish caught in this fashion before. The rod dipped, and then he pulled back on it, gently and slowly, backing awkwardly up the bank. This operation he repeated several times, until he reached out and pulled in the line itself, letting the rod fall onto the ground beside him. In doing this, he stepped rapidly down the bank and then quite into the water. He pulled hand over hand on the line. He was rewarded when he reached the end and held up a shining silver fish, which flipped desperately as he held it out of the water. He stepped back onto the shore and hit the fish sharply on the head, using a stone the size of a man's fist.

After that blow, the fish lay still. Then the boy worked the hook out of its mouth, laid his rod on the grassy bank and turned to grin at me. "My first today. My first for three days. How do you like that?"

He had a round face and a large smile. He wore overalls, a plain shirt, no shoes, and his arms and face were browned. His hair was yellow, bleached almost white. He stepped up to the road, wiped his right hand on the overalls and held it out to me. "I'm Oliver McWilliams. You're staying with old Dan Thiel, but I don't know your name."

"Jean Wainwright," I shook his hand. "How do you do, Oliver."

He grimaced. "Don't call me that. Call me Mac. Everybody does. I don't know what my parents were thinking of to name me Oliver. They say it has dignity and I'll be grateful for it later, but I don't believe that for a minute. The fights I have had about it."

"With your parents? Why should you fight with parents about a name."

"No, with fellows. I'm a student at the Phillips Academy at Exeter, and with a name like Oliver you can get in a lot of fights there, let me tell you. I would have liked something simple, like John or Samuel, something more peaceful. *Your* parents certainly knew what they were doing."

"Thank you," I said. I had little experience in conversing with boys, so I couldn't be sure that he meant to compliment me, but I decided that the wisest course was to act as if he were.

"What kind of fish is that?" I asked.

"Don't you know? A trout. I'll have it for supper tonight, and another if I can catch it. Would you like to try?"

"No, thank you," I said. "But I would like to watch. If I may."

"Sure, have a seat. That's strange though."

"Why?"

37

"Most girls wouldn't want to watch a fellow fish."

"Why not?"

"Who knows? Probably the same reason why most fellows wouldn't care to watch a girl sew a seam."

"Have you ever seen someone sew a seam?"

"Sure, my mother."

"I've never seen anyone fish before, not like this." I sat down and watched while he impaled a worm on the hook and tossed the line into the river. He bent to pick up the rod, and then sat down himself, below me and to the left, toward the bridge. "The trout stay near the shade under the bridge," he explained.

"I've seen fishing boats," I said, so that I wouldn't seem entirely ignorant, "and men fishing from the bridges into the Charles River."

"Where's that?"

"Where I live, in Cambridge. That's near Boston."

"I know."

It was odd, speaking to the back of his head.

"What are you doing here?" he asked. "Are you related to Mr. Thiel?"

"No, I'm working for him."

He turned his head and stared at me. "Working for him? Doing what? How old are you?"

"Twelve. Well . . . almost thirteen."

"I'm almost fourteen," Mac said. He looked cross. "My father won't let me work. I'd like to get a job on a farm. I'm strong enough. But my father says we don't need the money and there are people who do. Besides, I'm supposed to catch up on my geometry and Latin this summer. I'm behind in them. They're awfully complicated things, geometry and Latin."

I just nodded my head. I had studied both and understood the difficulties.

"What work do you do up there?" he asked.

"I'm cataloguing some papers," I told him, making it sound as important as I could. "Family papers," I added.

"Does he pay you?"

"Yes."

"I suppose you need the money. Are your parents . . ." He looked for a word. ". . . needy?"

"I'm an orphan. I live with my aunt."

"That's all right then," he said.

I wanted him to know that it was not need but my own ability that earned me the job. "My aunt is headmistress of a school in Cambridge. A school for girls. Mr. Thiel wrote her and asked if she knew anybody who could do the work."

"What happened to your parents?" he asked.

"I don't know," I replied.

"How can you not know?" he asked, then he turned red under his tan and quickly changed the subject. "My father is the doctor here. We came up from New Haven. We've only lived here five years."

"He's not Dr. Carter, is he?" I remembered how Mrs. Bywall had spoken of the doctor.

"That old horse doctor? Not a chance. Father practices *medicine*. Carter—well, he didn't. We came here just after he died. Father bought his practice."

"I've heard something about Dr. Carter from Mrs. Bywall the housekeeper."

"She was in prison."

"I know."

"What's she like? Does she talk about jail? Nobody ever sees her. People still sometimes talk about her, but nobody talks *to* her. Although they seem to feel sorry for her. The parents say she's not fit company for children."

"Do your parents say that?"

"Not in so many words. They don't agree, but they don't disagree either. Aah, it's a small town, Marlborough. People

39

here don't have much to talk about so they talk too much about things that they don't know about. And the Callenders—well, they keep their distance up on the hill. Maybe if they didn't, people wouldn't talk. But then they'd just find someone else to talk about—maybe even *me*—so I shouldn't complain. But it's interesting how they feel about strangers. Old Dan Thiel is a local man. They don't say much about him. But they don't think much good of him."

I wanted to ask this boy what they did say, but I didn't want to gossip. Also, I didn't know whether he could be trusted to tell the truth. I missed Aunt Constance's advice. I knew that she would have let me know whether or not Mac was a boy I could ask questions of. Perhaps I could write to ask whether she thought he was. But what could she tell from just my descriptions?

"You must be smart to have work like that," Mac said. "I've seen you, you know."

"Seen me?" This alarmed me, because I'd never seen him before. "Where?"

"I can track like an Indian," he said. "I've followed you."

"I don't believe it," I said.

"You wouldn't hear a bear coming after you." He laughed. "Your favorite spot is the waterfall," he added to prove his point.

I was speechless. He had been spying on me and I hadn't known. I felt my face grow hot. And I was angry. "What a low and sneaky thing to do."

"I've told you, haven't I?" The back of his neck, however, grew red.

"It's still sneaky." I thought for a minute. "I know Latin," I announced.

"And geometry too, I guess," he said sarcastically.

"I've begun geometry. I can translate Caesar."

"Hogwash." He stared at the water. He jiggled his rod.

"Suit yourself," I said and stood up. "But I could probably help you study." I don't know why I added that; just for extra meanness I'm afraid.

"I don't need any help," he answered, his back still to me. Then he turned around again and smiled at me, with his mouth and eyes. "That's a lie. I'm hopeless at it. And it *was* sneaky. Next time I'll tell you, if I'm there. All you do is read or moon around anyway. Once"—he grinned—"you were dancing."

I didn't know how to react. It was horrid to think you were alone and to find out that you weren't. "Why should I dance?" I demanded.

"No reason. It wasn't too bad, for a dance."

I said nothing.

He shrugged. "But listen, there's something else. I think somebody else was there too. Watching you."

He did not seem to be teasing; his face was serious. Somebody else there? Did he mean to frighten me with tales of ghosts? "I don't believe in spirits," I said.

"No, not that bosh. Across the brook, behind the trees, I thought I saw—something. Somebody. Who didn't what to be seen and was pretty good himself at tracking. If there *was* anybody there."

"Why should anybody spy on me?"

"It could be another boy, like me. But nobody goes near the Callender property. At least, nobody I know of, and I think I'd know. There's a shallow ford above the falls so I went to look. I saw a footprint, a boot footprint. Well, it might have been my imagination, it might not have been a footprint. That's pretty rocky ground there. It was just a couple of days ago, it was just a shadow moving. Father says my imagination runs away with me. He says I'm not a reliable witness."

"How can I learn to tell if people are spying?"

"Oh, I could teach you."

At that moment, Mr. Thiel returned. Mac put down his rod and scrambled up the bank to shake his hand. "How are you, sir?" he said.

"I'm well," Mr. Thiel replied.

Mac grinned at him, undaunted by his forbidding expression. "Father will be pleased. He says the highest tribute a doctor can receive is a six-month period with only childbeds to attend, and the odd broken arm."

"So you've met Jean," Mr. Thiel said.

"Yes."

"How do you like her?"

They spoke as if I were not there.

"She seems all right. She's probably smart."

"That's why she's here. You might come visit her some day, if you liked. She has no other company."

Mac nodded warily. "I might."

"Of an afternoon. We work in the mornings."

"Yes, sir."

"Jean, we should return now." Mr. Thiel finally looked at me. I started walking back, without waiting for him. He caught up with me easily and said, "It's good you met him."

I didn't answer. I would decide that for myself.

"You might enjoy some youthful companionship," he said.

Finally I spoke. "He seems to be one of the few people around here who will speak with you, so I guess you would approve of him." I was silent all the rest of the way to the house.

Chapter Five

By the time we reached the house I was thoroughly ashamed of myself. The long, silent walk had given me more than enough time to swallow my anger and recall my manners. What of it if Mr. Thiel had been ungracious? That did not excuse my own rudeness. As I tidied myself for dinner, I determined to make my apology. Aunt Constance had taught me that unpleasant tasks must be got out of the way briskly. That was her word, *briskly*, and I liked it because it sounded like a new broom, energetically sweeping away.

As soon as we were alone in the dining room, with full plates before us, I made my speech. "Mr. Thiel, I apologize for my rudeness. What I said was inexcusable. I should not have said it, and I am sorry for doing so." That done, I began to eat.

You can imagine my surprise when I heard him start to

laugh. He did not laugh loud or long, but the short barks of sound were clearly laughter.

"Accepted," he said, and just as I recognized that his smile occupied his face fully, it disappeared. He resumed his natural expression. "Probably, you would say I owe you an apology myself."

"Accepted," I said.

"Now, tell me something. You spoke rudely, yes, but did you speak untruthfully?"

He might have been teasing me. I tried to study his face. The face was severe and craggy, his dark glance sharp under forbidding eyebrows.

"Untruthfully? I cannot say that, because I really don't know, do I? You do live a very solitary life. I spoke as I thought, as things appear to me."

That satisfied him. "Mac runs wild here. If you would rather not share his company, I will tell him so."

"Oh no," I said quickly. "I've never known a boy."

"One of your Aunt Constance's prejudices?" he asked.

"I don't think so. We just have no opportunity to meet boys. Mac appears knowledgeable—about certain things."

"A wild Indian's knowledge," Mr. Thiel remarked.

"All knowledge is useful, don't you think?" I said.

"No, I don't." His effort to cut off conversation did not stop my tongue.

"You cannot understand what you do not know," I pointed out to him. "And if you cannot understand it, how can you make changes for the better?"

"You're a reformer," he said. Obviously, he did not care for reformers.

"I would like to be useful in the world," I answered. That was true. But there was something more I wanted, that I could not define. "There is something very wrong in Mrs. Bywall's life. It should not have happened that way," I finished lamely.

"Should," he repeated, as if that were a particularly silly word.

"I can't explain," I said. "But you seem to have felt it too. Why else is she here?"

"Because she does her job well," he said. "Because, as you pointed out earlier this afternoon, she would take the job, which no other person in the village would have done."

"Mr. Thiel," I said, feeling very clever, "you do not like to be accused of doing a good deed."

"Not if I don't deserve it," he answered.

That evening I wrote to Aunt Constance, describing Marlborough and Mr. Thiel's home and reporting to her about my progress with the Callender papers. I described how I had gone about it, and how I planned to distinguish categories; then I asked for her response and her suggestions. I told her how I spent the days and tried to explain my feeling for the glade by the waterfall. It was a long letter. I was reluctant to end it because while I was writing I had the feeling that Aunt Constance was nearby.

The next afternoon I set off on my own to take the letter to the post office. I deliberately avoided telling Mr. Thiel of my intention, although I don't know why. I did, however, inform Mrs. Bywall. Someone should know. Besides, I thought she would notice if I was not there.

"Are you sure you can manage it, the walk?" she asked. We were washing up the luncheon dishes. Then she answered herself. "Of course you can. You're as I used to be, thin but strong. In prison, we did laundry and more laundry, and what with that and the diet—if you could call it that. . . . But I used to be slender and wiry, like you. Have you money for the stamp?"

"Yes, I still have my traveling money," I said. I dried my hands and prepared to leave.

"Miss Jean," Mrs. Bywall said, wiping her own hands on her apron. Then she left the room abruptly. I waited. I did not know why or what for. No change of expression on her impassive face had prepared me for her departure.

Mrs. Bywall returned carrying a simple gingham dress. She stood awkwardly before me.

"Is that for me?" I asked.

"If you want it," she said. "Not to say there's anything wrong with what you have."

"Thank you," I said. I didn't know if I should reach out to take it or wait to have it given to me.

"I had this bit of material, and if you wanted something cooler, I thought, we're not very fancy around here. . . ." She stopped speaking.

"I could wear it today," I offered.

"Suit yourself," she answered. It was the oddest kindness I had ever been offered, and I was not sure how to respond, so I simply thanked her again.

The dress fit well enough. It was made to fall loosely, like a smock, and shorter than any of my other dresses. The hem fell just above my ankle. Wearing it, I felt free to move about. I stopped to show Mrs. Bywall.

"It's what the girls around here wear," she said. "Of course, it wouldn't do for the city. The girls here often go without stockings and shoes too, for comfort."

"I'll be a wild Indian, like Oliver McWilliams." I essayed a smile, to which she did not respond. I had the ungrateful thought that Mr. Thiel had required her to make the dress, for reasons of his own.

"You might do worse," Mrs. Bywall said finally, dismissing me.

With the letter and a few pennies in my pinafore pocket, with a new dress and bare feet, I walked along the dirt roadway beside the stream. There was nobody on the lawn of the Callender house. The dirt under my feet felt soft and fine, the stones cut into my tender soles until I learned to avoid them. The short skirt was light around my legs. I did

46

feel half-wild. Sometimes, for no reason, I ran through the dappled sunlight, just for the pleasure of moving my arms and legs freely. When I arrived at the village, I looked around for Mac but did not see him. I turned toward the brick buildings.

The general store, where mail was collected, was easy to find as Marlborough had only the one street. The store had a sign, which announced itself, and added that E. Willy was the proprietor. I hesitated, wondering about my bare feet, then decided that if it were improper, Mrs. Bywall would not have advised me to go without shoes. I stepped into the building.

It was cool, dim. Shelves filled with dry goods and hardware filled the walls toward the front. The groceries were toward the back, canned goods and bags of rice, flour, coffee. The Franklin stove was not lit at this time of year, but it occupied a central place. Bottles of whiskey stood in a line directly behind a stocky man who was himself behind a counter. The usual jars of bright-colored penny candy were on one end of the counter.

I walked up to the man and said that I would like to mail a letter.

He answered not a word, but reached down a small scale from behind him. I gave him my letter.

"To Boston," he said. "To Miss Constance Wainwright," he said.

"How much is it please?"

He told me the price and I paid him. "You'll be staying up at Mr. Thiel's," he said.

"Yes."

"Then we'll not see you often," he said.

I said nothing, and he stared at me with bright, curious eyes. His hair was almost perfectly white, his face almost perfectly square. His skin was covered with small wrinkles. I did not like him. "You don't look like you come from the

Callender property," he remarked at last. "But looks can be deceiving." He waited for me to say something, but I didn't. "Will there be anything else?"

"No, thank you," I said. "Good day."

He did not answer, and I went back outside. I stood on the porch for a time, letting my eyes readjust to the sunlight, studying the white houses on the other side of the dirt road. Then I stepped down onto the dusty street and saw Mac approaching the other side of the bridge. I walked toward him, waving to catch his attention, when someone hurrying out of the other building ran into me from the side.

A pair of hands took me by the shoulders to keep me from falling into the dusty road. Before I could properly appreciate what had happened, a voice began apologizing: "How could I have been so clumsy? I'm so sorry—are you all right? Yes, I think so, perhaps a little bemused, but you don't look as if you're hurt. *Are* you hurt? Is that a pained or a puzzled expression? I do apologize. Please say you'll forgive me. It was clumsy of me, I wasn't watching, and the sunlight after the dark interior light is blinding, don't you think? I've always thought so. I wish you'd talk to me, just anything, so I can hear if I've hurt you. But I'm not giving you much of a chance, am I?"

It was Enoch Callender who stood beside me, concern in eyes, which were of blue as bright as the sky. The sun shone off of his golden hair. His face looked contrite and amused and curious, all at once; the exact expressions changing so fast I couldn't see when they flowed into one another. He wore a white suit, spotless. "I'm perfectly fine," I assured him. "Really." I felt myself flushing under his scrutiny. "It's unmannerly to stare," I told him, as if he had been one of the little girls in my charge. Then I regretted my own ill-mannered tongue. But he smiled mishcievously at me.

"I'm not usually clumsy. And I'm not in the habit of

trampling down young ladies on public thoroughfares. Say you will forgive me." He smiled as if he was sure I would.

"There is nothing to forgive," I said. "Truly."

"I'm relieved to hear you say that." He took off his straw hat and bowed elaborately to me. "Let me introduce myself less precipitously. Enoch Challender, at your service."

"I know."

He smiled again. He seemed to know immediately that I did not mean my words to sound as curt as they did. "Know what? Know I am at your service?" I answered with a smile. "Or why need we two lie to one another, is that what you mean? You're an unusually direct sort of young lady and I tell you straight out I like that. Of course, I do know who you are. We all heard, as soon as you'd arrived. You're staying at Dan's house, Dan Thiel. They say you are cataloging the family papers. My family, of course. Are they dreadfully dull? I'm afraid they must be. I shall have to apologize for that too. My father was a dreadfully dull old man, if I do say so myself. All those fusty hours turning over the yellowed pages—no, I don't envy you the job. A double apology then, Miss—no wait, you mustn't tell me, and I see in your face that you are not hastening to do so—are you also discreet? Truly, a rare character, truly good luck that I—so to speak"—he smiled broadly, doffing his hat again—"ran into you. Ah, good, you have a sense of humor. I wonder if you'll allow me to play a little game I like. It's so important to have diversions for the mind."

I didn't know what to say, so stood looking up into his face.

"Are you returning to the big house? Shall we walk together? I'm incredibly trustworthy, you will be safe with me."

"Don't we go up on opposite sides of the river?" I asked.

"There is a way across. It's something of a secret, but I'll share it with you. It's not a large secret—I can see you would disapprove of my telling you large secrets on such a short acquaintance. It's a modest little private arrangement, really. You'll be disappointed by it, but I'll tell you anyway now that I've piqued your curiosity." I had no time to open my mouth to say that I wasn't at all curious; he talked on without waiting. "We can cross over at the falls. You didn't know that, did you? I'll like surprising you, I can see that. You will have to walk a little further, but I would enjoy the time in your company. I would enjoy it very much."

He too would have to walk farther, which I did not say. Instead, I agreed that we might walk together. I didn't see how I could refuse, and I preferred walking side by side to standing facing him in the middle of the street. Somehow, looking directly at him distracted me—his face held such liveliness and he spoke so fluently. This liveliness, the quick energy of him, was something I had never met with before in an adult. Already, I had a sense of unpredictability, as if all of life was a game, which he very much enjoyed playing. We moved up the road and over the little bridge. Mac had begun to fish and did not meet my eye. Mr. Callender talked on. "I was speaking of my little game. I'm really rather good at it. You may thing I'm blowing my own horn, but I always say if you don't think well of yourself, then who will? And we see so few strangers—strangers are a rare commodity in Marlborough—that I always ask the privilege of those I meet. So I ask the privilege of you, my nameless young lady."

"Yes, but what is it?"

"You have humor as well; really, I can't tell you how glad I am we met. However inopportunely it came about—I am not forgetting my part in all of this. But to the point. I have a theory that it is possible to tell a person's name from his appearance. The person must be of mature age, that goes without saying. But I believe that in that circumstance the

50

astute observer can guess the name. So I'll guess at your name—unless you object?"

I shook my head, greatly amused. I could think of no reason to object to his foolishness, and I was curious about what he would guess.

"This name must be pretty, but not fancified. Something solid. Something with a streak of the practical, but a hint of vision as well. Simple and feminine, but with the possibility of—if I'm right—sternness."

Nobody had ever said all those things about me. I had not forgotten Mr. Thiel calling me an "odd little niece." It was pleasant now to be so approved of. I waited for the game to continue. We were on a wagon track on the opposite side of the river, and the trees grew so thickly that I would not have guessed, if I hadn't known, that there was a drive on the opposite side. Thickly-leaved branches made it shady and pleasant as we walked along. "I think," he said after some silent thought, "if I were to name you, I'd call you Diana, after the goddess of the moon."

I lifted my eyes to his, to tell him how wrong he was, but he raised his hand to silence me. "No, that's not my guess, now that I see it would be wrong. Something more sensible, Charlotte, or Jane. No, Jean. Yes, I *like* that. Here is my formal guess—Jean. Now you can tell me, what is your name? *Is* it Jean? Or any variation of that? You've got to give me a little leeway."

It was astounding. I could only nod my head.

He lifted his face to the trees and crowed with delight. "I told you I was good at it, didn't I? Now you believe me. You thought I was being foolish, but I wasn't, was I? Of course, I wouldn't know your last name."

"Wainwright."

"How do you do Miss Wainwright? But I may call you Jean, mayn't I? After all, I just named you myself."

"But how do you do it?" I asked.

"Ah—that is a secret. What would you have guessed for me? Not Enoch, of course, that's much to sharp and hard, much too stern and Biblical. I'm named after my grandfather—something of a rogue, whom the name Enoch suited as little as it does me. If you were guessing, what would you name me?"

"I need to think carefully about that," I answered. This was not true. I knew immediately I would have named him something strong and handsome, like Lancelot, or perhaps mischievous, like Robin, after Robin Goodfellow.

"You're right," he agreed, as we passed on through the silent woods. "It does take careful thought. I do wish my father had been a man given to careful thought. I like that phrase. Careful thought. Most things do become clearer with its aid. More clear than people think," he said. "However, I'm wandering off the subject. I do wander, I must warn you. Shall I tell you all about myself? Or would you rather be the first to tell? Since we're going to be friends."

"You," I said. He could not possibly be interested in me.

"I am old Dan's brother-in-law. Mr. Thiel, that is. One must speak respectfully of one's relatives. More precisely, I was his brother-in-law. My sister Irene was his wife. She has been dead these ten years." When he spoke of his sister, his voice had no laughter, and his eyes grew serious. "Irene raised me because my mother died bringing me into the world. I often wonder what it would have been like to have had a mother; a mother is a terrible thing to miss. A child who has no mother I think deserves all the sympathy people have to give. Irene spoiled me, everyone said so, and I have to agree with them. It was wonderful. Here I am thirty-eight years old. I don't look it, do I? A gilded youth, that's what I look like. I have no occupation and am what in better days, in more elegant times, would have been called a gentleman. I have three children. Joseph is seventeen, and is perhaps too much like me. Victoria is fifteen and growing into quite a beauty. She should do well for herself, if we could just get her out of this village and into a respectable society. Then there is Benjamin, who at fourteen may be anything. I haven't insulted your age, have I? How old are you?"

"Twelve," I said. "Thirteen in the fall."

"I'd have guessed that," he said. "Now you know all about me, you must tell me about yourself."

"I live with my Aunt Constance, who was, I believe, a friend of your sister's."

He thought about that. "I've never heard of her. Of course, Irene had any number of friends about whom I knew nothing. For several years, we lived very separate lives, when I was away at school, and then after I married. Irene did have secret leanings toward the suffragettes. Could your aunt be one of those?"

"Of course," I said. "Aunt Constance says it is utterly unreasonable to deny women the vote; if you think carefully about it, you must see that women are as able as men. The major difference is—of course—education. She thinks women should be as educated as men. She has her own school in Cambridge. That is how I come to be here. Mr. Thiel is on the Board of Governors of the Academy."

"Is he now?" Mr. Callender said, as if that surprised him. "What about your parents?"

"I know nothing about them."

"But surely your aunt must have told you something."

"No, nothing."

"Don't you find that strange? If you are the child of her sister or brother, she should want to talk to you of your family. Unless of course—" he glanced quickly at me and stopped speaking. His meaning was clear.

"She will tell me when it is right for me to know," I said. But he had inserted a tiny grain of doubt. Why hadn't she told me? Was she keeping me in ignorance of some shameful secret?

"Ah, well, that may make a difference, of course. There are so many curious things that happen in the world, aren't there? At least you seem to trust your Aunt Constance, which speaks well of her."

"Yes of course."

"And where do you live?"

"In Cambridge, near Boston," I repeated.

"You're a city child then? I was myself and it's a rare privilege, don't you agree? My city was New York. Do you know New York?"

I did not.

"I was born there and lived all my life there until my father moved us up here. Have you read about that yet in those papers you are trudging through?"

"I have noticed that he didn't approve of the munitions factory."

"He didn't approve of much, my father. He didn't approve of the munitions factory, he didn't approve of the war, he didn't approve of the way his own father kept him out of the army. The old man paid one of his employees three hundred dollars to enlist in place of my father. It was perfectly legal, and generous compared to what other men were getting for the same job. But my father didn't approve. My father also didn't approve of gambling, drinking, swearing, of eating too well or sleeping too much. He didn't approve of pleasure. I have always suspected that he didn't approve of life."

I giggled.

"But then my father didn't know much about life. At the first honest blow old lady life handed him, he died. His heart just refused to beat under the circumstances. Almost as if he said to himself, 'If this is what it is, I will have nothing to do with it.'"

"What happened?" I asked, bold again.

"My sister died, under curious circumstances. Actually, she died after he did, but it was clear she would go. It's a pity she didn't die first, it made a terrible muddle. However, die she did, and although it was unpleasant, we have all come through it, because Callenders, true Callenders, survive. You'll notice that in those papers. And Dan Thiel has made quite a good thing out of it."

We walked a way in silence. The river ran beside us, going in the opposite direction. As we went uphill, great boulders began to appear, as if they had forced their way up through concealing earth, like the earth's secrets forcing their way into daylight.

"How do you and Dan Thiel get on then?" Mr. Callender asked after a while.

"Satisfactorily."

Mr. Callender threw back his head and laughed. "And I know what that means. It means he goes out to his shed and paints, while you rustle through dusty papers."

There was enough truth in that not to be contradicted.

"You are a diplomat, Miss Jean Wainwright," Mr. Callender said. "Will you wait for my son Joseph and marry him and make a good man of him? He needs a cautious head beside his own. Will you propose yourself to save him?"

"I would not be a good match," I said.

"There is that," Mr. Callender agreed, "because an heiress would solve many of our problems. But the native habitat of heiresses is not such places as Marlborough, is it? No, it's the cities." He spread his arms out as if to encompass an invisible world. "I do *miss* the city. The variety most of all, it's like—there's nothing like it, is there?"

He told me of the New York he remembered from his childhood, as we walked on up the hill toward his house. He could describe the seaport of New York so vividly that I almost saw it: the tall-masted ships, the sailors of different origins and colors. The sense of the whole world, gathered together in one place, the variety of it, the movement, the color. He spoke of New York as one familiar with all of its aspects.

"I was lucky to live so many years there. I'll try to look on the bright side. No reason not to is there? I had many happy years there. Father didn't dare sell the factory until Grandfather was safely dead. Father was a good businessman, surprisingly enough; at least he made money. But as soon as the old man died he closed the factory down. It seems that Father had the ability to be a successful businessman but not the courage. Don't you think?"

I wouldn't have known, and said so.

"I won't complain. It's a sizable fortune he left, although it's a Gordian knot at this point. Someday—" he said. He did not finish the sentence. "And what will you do with your life, Jean?"

I told him of my plans to further my education and then become, myself, an educator. He admired them, he said.

These conversations took us to his own house, where nobody stirred behind the white curtains on the windows to see us as we walked by at the foot of the lawn. "It's the second best, of course," he said, "but comfortable enough for us." We went on up to the waterfall. I was sorry we had come to the end of our walk.

"Now," Mr. Callender said, with an air of mystery, like a magician about to perform some sleight-of-hand, "I am going to show you something only known to one living person. Myself. It was a secret between Irene and me. I must tell you about Irene someday. You've got a gift for listening, you must know that."

He reached high up into an old beech tree and pulled

down a long gray board. "Did you ever see anything like this?" he asked.

"It looks like a jumping board," I said. "We have one in our garden. The little girls bounce on it."

"You can do that with this too," Mr. Callender said. He lifted it over his head and, standing close to the edge of the ravine, let it fall to the other side. "We used it for a bridge, Irene and I. Mr. Thiel was not one of my most ardent admirers, shall we say? So Irene and I met secretly sometimes. I enjoyed the game, as I enjoy all games. It will make a handy bridge for you, won't it?"

The board was narrow. The falls, beneath it now, looked dangerous.

"I'll steady it with my weight on this side," Mr. Callender said. He stood on the end of the board, near the edge of the ravine. "It's secure now. Here, you steady it and I'll cross. It's not nearly as hazardous as it looks."

I stood on the end. He walked out to the middle, surefooted as a cat. At the center, where the drop was long enough to require extra caution, he began to bounce gently, his arms outstretched for balance. The board under my feet responded. "Isn't that dangerous?" I called.

He turned around and walked back to where I stood, his eyes mischievous. "Life is dangerous. How tedious life would be without some danger to wake us up. I wouldn't have taken you for a coward," he said.

Of course, at that I had to walk across boldly, as if my heart were not in my throat, as if I were not frightened of falling off the narrow board into the water below, which foamed around boulders beneath me. It was with relief that I stepped off onto the other side; I disguised it as best I could.

Mr. Callender drew the board back and replaced it in the same tree. "Will you come dine with us on a Sunday?" he called.

"I would like that," I called back.

"That's good, because I know someone who won't." Mr. Callender grinned. "Until we meet again, Jean Wainwright." He raised his hat to me.

I waved and made my way across the glade. Mr. Callender became quickly invisible among the trees opposite, and even though I listened well I could hear no sound of his footsteps. I was recalling to myself our long walk and the conversation, when an unbidden memory came to my mind: this man, whom I had been so easily making friends with, was responsible for sending Mrs. Bywall to prison. The idea was unpleasant to me. I determined to find out more about what had happened. I knew little about either of the people concerned, except that of the two, Mr. Callender seemed more frank, less secretive.

Chapter Six

As I was returning to the house, trying to recall a turn of phrase Mr. Callender used, trying to determine what it was about him that made him so easy to converse with, I met with Mr. Thiel walking back from some pasture; burly and strong he looked, like a countryman, not a painter. His boots were coated with mud, his hair matted with sweat.

"Look at you," he said. I could have said the same to him but refrained. His presence cast shadows over my mood, but I would not let that dominate my spirits. "Mrs. Bywall made the dress for me." I thought he might remark on the alteration in my appearance, but he chose not to. He waited without speaking for me to catch up with him.

"I've just come from her father's house. They farm this property for me, her parents and the two brothers."

"I didn't know that."

"It looks to be a good year," he went on. "The corn is

coming up nicely. I hear you've been to the village this afternoon."

"How did you know that?"

"Young McWilliams told me."

"It would be hard to keep a secret around here," I observed.

He thought about that. "Some secrets seem impossible to keep. Others, no. I told Mac to come calling tomorrow. It's going to rain. I advised him to bring his Latin book."

I was silent.

"You're not going to get angry at me again, are you? You have no cause."

I supposed he was right. I had, after all, told him I wanted to know Mac. "No. I did see him in the village but we didn't speak." Apparently, though, he had come running up to find Mr. Thiel, when it had looked to me as if he were settling in to fish all afternoon. I didn't care for that at all. "How do you know it will rain?" I asked, to change the subject.

"Matt Jenkins told me, and he's seldom wrong. He says we're in for two or three days of it."

I looked up at a blue sky between thickly leaved branches of trees. A few white puffy clouds blew across it. "It doesn't look like rain to me."

I don't know why I put off telling Mr. Thiel that I had met Enoch Callender, whether it was some instinct that it would not please my employer, or some desire to hold a secret to myself a little while. I did tell him at dinner. When he heard, he looked at me sharply. "How did you like him?" he asked at last, as if he knew he should say something but was reluctant to talk on the subject.

"I liked him very much," I began, and then went on to relate our conversation about New York. I made quite a little speech. Mr. Thiel sat listening, watching me darkly without moving. I did not tell him that Mr. Callender had guessed at my name and guessed correctly, amusing as that was. That seemed the kind of frivolity of which Mr. Thiel would not approve. But I did ask him if he would tell me what had happened, when Mrs. Bywall had been imprisoned.

"I can't see why you need to know that," he said, and said no more. I deduced that he had refused my request and put it out of my mind. I was therefore quite surprised when he instructed me to join him in his sitting room as we rose from the table.

It was Mr. Thiel's habit to retire to his sitting room and to stay there until after I had gone upstairs. I spent the evenings washing up with Mrs. Bywall, then reading in my own room upstairs. I could not tell what this change in the ordinary course of things meant.

Mr. Thiel's room, at the rear of the house, was still lit by the setting sun and filled with pink-gold bars of light. It was a small room, furnished with only a drawing table and two armchairs drawn up beside the small fireplace. The walls were paneled. One oil painting hung over the fireplace. Mrs. Bywall brought me in a pot of tea, with a pitcher of milk, a bowl of sugar, and a cup, on a tray. On another tray, already waiting by one of the chairs, a bottle of brandy and a snifter and a cigar box were set out. The most interesting thing in the bare room was the painting. I was not sure if I was supposed to notice it, or if I was not allowed to look. I tried to ignore it.

"Go ahead," Mr. Thiel said, apparently noticing my curiosity. So I walked up to the fireplace to study it closely. As I suspected, it was his own work, signed in the lower corner: D. Thiel, 1887. I don't know how to describe it. It was a strong painting, beautiful but also harsh. It was clear in color and line, but not an exact pictorial representation.

Mr. Thiel apparently knew my glade by the falls. He had painted it in the light of a setting sun, and I recognized it as much by its mood as its physical appearance. He understood the serenity of it, as I understood it. But in the shadows of the trees, in the dark water, something frightening hid itself. It was as if the growing darkness groped to take over the peaceful beauty of the scene. I stood a long time before that painting.

"You know the place?" he asked finally.

"Yes," I said. "Do you ever paint people?"

"Seldom," he said. "I can't paint them as I understand them. Once or twice I've tried, without much success. There are contradictions, ambiguities. . . ."

I stood, looking at him, looking back to the picture. For the first time in all the years I'd known him, he sounded unsure of exactly what he thought.

"You don't have to say anything," he said.

"I like it," I said, knowing what a meaningless remark it was.

"That doesn't matter, does it?" he asked abruptly.

"Perhaps not," I said. "It's very—strong."

"Yes. However, sit down now. Maybe another time you'd like to look around the studio. Maybe another time I'd like to allow you."

That was not exactly a warm invitation. I sat in a chair, poured myself a cup of tea, sweetened it and waited. He picked out a cigar and leaned back. "So you like Mr. Enoch Callender," he said at last.

"Yes." I couldn't think of any reason to deny the truth.

"And you want to find excuses for him," he said. I did not answer that, although it was equally true. "I'll tell you what I know, which you can believe or not, as you choose."

There was no reason for me to respond; he left me with nothing to say.

"The Jenkinses, Mrs. Bywall's family, have always lived in Marlborough. They had three sons and five daughters. Mrs. Bywall is the oldest daughter, the third child. They were not poor, but they had no money to spare. Jenkins did not own his own land, but farmed that of other people as a tenant. The entire family worked hard to keep things going. Two of the sons married and moved away, one younger daughter went into service in Northampton, and Mrs. Bywall went to work for the Enoch Callenders. This was when she had just married their young farmhand, Charlie Bywall." He bit off the end of a cigar, then lit it. He stared at his own picture as he spoke.

"Now the Callenders were the great family hereabouts. They were rich. They lived well. They weren't natives to the area so the villagers saw them—still see them—as outsiders, untrustworthy, unknown. But their coming made the village more prosperous so everyone was eager to please them. The Jenkinses didn't want their daughter working for the Callenders, but they had no choice. Mrs. Bywall could earn more money there than in any other way, little as it was. She worked as a housemaid, which meant she did everything: taking care of the children, cleaning, laundering, serving at table, kitchen chores. They overworked her, of course, and took advantage of her need for the work.

"Mrs. Bywall had a genuine need. Her young brother was ill, probably with consumption, and there were medicines that needed to be bought and the doctor to be paid."

"Dr. Carter," I said.

"Yes. A fool and a grasping man. For the poorer folk he had a unique system of payment: pay first, then get medical service. He was well hated. He had made too many mistakes: not recognizing appendicitis or setting a broken arm so that it left a man permanently crippled. But he was the only doctor available. Nobody went to him unless they were desperate. The Jenkinses were desperate. The boy coughed blood."

I nodded my head.

"Jenkins could have gone elsewhere for help but he was

proud. He had friends who would have helped out gladly, if they had known."

He was off the subject so I asked, "But what did Mrs. Bywall do?"

"She stole some silver teaspoons. At the trial there was no question of that, she never lied about her guilt."

"But they caught her. So they had the spoons back, didn't they?"

"Enoch Callender insisted on prosecuting the case."

"Why?"

"He never confided in me. His father and his sister tried to dissuade him. That may be why. He argued that when respect for property declines, the legal and social shape of the world is endangered. He said he must do the right thing. He said it caused him pain to do so."

Mr. Thiel's face was hidden in shadows. "You don't sound as if you believed that," I said. Those struck me as good reasons.

"Doing the right thing," he answered. "I don't know about a phrase like that. My own history . . . I wonder if I can be said to have done the right thing."

"You mean during the war?"

"Your aunt told you? Of course she would. I still think I did the only possible thing, but was it the right thing? In any case, Enoch Callender did the right thing, and Mrs. Bywall was sent to prison. That was 1880 and she was sixteen. The year before I had married Irene Callender, which is how I come to know a little more about the affair."

"What more?" I asked.

"That Josiah Callender, my father-in-law, argued with his son about his actions. That when Enoch wouldn't change his mind, his father paid for a defense attorney from Boston. That afterwards he did everything possible to help the Jenkins boy. To no avail." So the Callenders had helped after all, as Enoch Callender must have known they would.

64

"But I'm a native here myself," Mr. Thiel said, interrupting my thoughts. "I had known Florence Bywall since she was a girl, a child. So I know what prison did to her." His voice was so cold I felt a sudden chill.

"She is only thirty years old," I said. I had been working it out.

"The life aged her. Prisons," he said, and then stopped. "Of course when Charlie ran away—"

"How long after was that?"

"Almost a year."

"He certainly didn't wait very long." I was indignant.

"The boy died," Mr. Thiel continued.

"Poor Mrs. Bywall," I said.

"And of course, since she had been in prison, people would have little to do with her when she returned. They sympathized with her, but from a safe distance."

"What a terrible thing. What about you? What did you do?"

"What I had to do with it needn't concern you," he said sharply. It was as if I had reminded him of who he was, and who I was. "That is the story you've asked to hear. I don't know what you will make of it."

"I will have to think carefully about it," I told him. I did not think the Enoch Callender who had been so entertaining and so kind to me would have acted with the capricious cruelty Mr. Thiel hinted at. I wondered if my employer had kept silent about something he preferred to keep secret. His dark face gave me no clue.

The next day it rained, just as Mr. Thiel had predicted. The rain poured down out of a gray sky, pounding on the roof, splashing on the ground. It was a steady, hard, stubborn rain. As was my custom, I worked during the morning. I was beginning to understand what a difference there was between Josiah Callender and his father, Enoch.

Enoch had sent Josiah to Paris while the War Between the States was raging. Josiah had not wanted to go, but had not been able to successfully oppose his father. The old man had an iron will, it seemed. Josiah was thirty-five at the time, widowed, the father of two children, and still his father had packed him off to Europe like a boy. "I'll square things here," the old man had written, "and you just be sure to hire a competent nurse for my grandchildren. Hire a British woman, not a foreigner. I'll hear no more of your plaints, do you understand that? If I can deal with what people say here, then surely, at such a distance, your delicate conscience can survive. Most won't blame you, I daresay." When Josiah wrote from London to protest again, his father answered, "Anything you could do would be useless. You had better face that. You wouldn't fight. How would it serve your children for you to be in jail? You are my heir, Josiah, and you have a duty to me."

After that exchange, Josiah's monthly letters concerned only the various capitals of Europe, the children, and the scenery. His father's rare answers dealt with the difficulties of running a munitions factory, restrictive government regulations and unreliable employees. This series of letters was most curious, like two people, each talking to himself, but both calling it a conversation.

After luncheon, Mac arrived, rain dripping off his hair, his Latin book kept dry by layers of newspaper. Mrs. Bywall showed him into the library. We had laid a small fire to take the damp chill out of the air. Even in July it can be chilly up in the Berkshires. I must admit I was glad to see Mac. I had worked hard all morning and felt the need of some diversion from the unfriendly relation between father and son and the endless household accounts. The Callenders, at that time, had returned to New York City. The war was over.

Mac looked around the room. His eyes traveled from the

papers on the table to the twelve boxes ranged about the floor and returned to me where I sat behind the large desk. "This must be hard work," he said. "It looks like you though."

"Whatever do you mean by that?" I asked. Sitting behind the desk, I reminded myself of Aunt Constance. Mac could have been a misbehaving student sent to me for correction.

"It's so tidy."

"Tidy?" I looked around at the awful mess.

"No, it is. I bet you know what is in every pile." He was right, I did. "And I bet you have done an awful lot of work already. How many of these boxes have you got through?"

"Two and a half," I said. It did not seem like many.

"How long have you been here?"

"Nearly two weeks," I said. Odd, it felt longer.

"Do you really want to help me with my Latin?" he asked. "I'm pretty hopeless."

"Don't be silly," I said, echoing Aunt Constance, "nobody is hopeless."

Together, we moved two boxes to clear a place before the fire. We sat on the floor there. He kept looking behind him.

"You're right," he said. "I probably couldn't do this job."

I discovered that I didn't like Mac to be humble. "No more could I work in the fields all day," I said. "Which is no credit to either of us."

He grinned then, and relaxed. "It'll rain tomorrow, too, and I'll take you to the falls. When it's rained for a day, they're . . . bigger," he finished lamely.

"I'd like that," I said. "Is the river swollen?"

"It's starting. By tomorrow it might flood a little, if it keeps up like this."

We went to work on the Latin. He was not hopeless, but he was woefully confused. We went over and over the early forms. Mac had a poor memory, that was true. He was also easily discouraged. So I encouraged him and helped him, just as if I were teaching one of Aunt Constance's youngest pupils to read.

Later Mrs. Bywall came in with a pot of cocoa and a plate of warm cookies. Both Mac and I were glad to be interrupted. We closed up the book and threw the crumpled exercise papers onto the fire.

"You seemed to be chattering away with Mr. Callender," Mac said. He devoured a cookie with one bite and reached out for two more. "Yesterday," he reminded me.

"Is there anything wrong with that?"

"What did you talk about?"

"Were you spying again? I don't like being spied on."

"I wasn't spying, I was fishing. Remember?" he said angrily. "You saw me. I saw him run into you on purpose."

"He didn't," I said. "It was an accident."

Mac shrugged. "I saw it. You didn't. What did you talk about?"

"Nothing that would interest you," I said. "You don't like him, do you?"

"Not a bit."

"Why?"

"I have my reasons."

"Well I do," I said. "He's a civilized person."

"He's a snake," Mac said.

"You're jealous," I said, feeling I had gained great insight.

"Jealous of him?" Mac was surprised. "Why should I be jealous of him?"

I could think of a number of reasons, but didn't feel right about stating them.

"If he's so great, why did he do what he did to Mrs. Bywall?" Mac continued.

"You didn't even live here than, so how do you know?" I retorted quickly.

"I just don't trust him."

"That is none of my concern," I said. We sat sulkily silent for a long time. I was sorry I'd quarreled with Mac about Mr. Callender because, when I took time to think about it, I realized that Mac might have been able to tell me more about that past history. I was not satisfied with what I had learned from Mr. Thiel the evening before.

At that time Mr. Thiel entered the room, fortunately, because I could not think of any way to end the quarrel and I wanted to end it.

Mr. Thiel's boots were muddy. He handed me a letter from Aunt Constance. "Hello Mac," he said. "Mrs. Bywall is bringing me a cup," he said, apparently to declare his intention of joining us. It was his house, so I couldn't object. "Did you learn Latin?" he asked, looking at my worktable as if to be sure I was earning my pay.

I let Mac talk to Mr. Thiel while I quickly read over Aunt Constance's letter. Then I rejoined them and listened to their conversation about the fishing, the crops, the weather, the possibility of floods.

Mac left soon after that, but he returned the next afternoon. After we had worked on the Latin, he took me to see the falls as he had promised. We were bundled up in macintoshes and huge hats, and we had to lean against the force of the wind as we ascended the steep hillside. We spoke little, because we had to yell to be heard. Every now and then Mac would turn and smile at me. His smile was contagious. It was obvious how much he enjoyed splashing through the puddles and the wet grasses. The rain came donw hard. Branches on the trees swayed in the wind. It was not dangerous, but exciting. I was enjoying myself.

When we came to the edge of the ravine, Mac got down on all fours and motioned that I was to do the same. I hesitated—a dress is not the most convenient article of clothing in which to crawl over wet, muddy ground—but followed his example. We crawled to the edge and looked over.

The water tumbled, poured, roared over the top of the falls. It thundered around the boulders, turbulent. The descending sheets of water crashed into the boulder-strewn pool at the foot, and the stream dashed away, swollen and impatient. Mac and I knelt there, silent, side by side.

A large branch, the size of a hoe handle, swept by us over the top of the falls. Falling, it was smashed and broken. The pieces reached the pool and swirled there among the foamy currents for a few seconds before they were seized by the water and carried down the stream.

I had not imagined the power of the falls in flood. It was exhilarating, but also frightening. We watched it for a long time. I knew that this place would never seem so innocently safe to me again, but I also knew this was another form of its beauty. After a time, Mac motioned me back under the shelter of the big beech trees, where the leaves and branches gave some protection from rain and wind.

"Well?" he asked.

"It reminds me of Mr. Thiel's picture," I told him. "Show me where you hide."

He pointed up into a beech set behind the first of them. "Up there," he said. "Mr. Thiel's picture?"

"He has a painting of the falls and the glade in his sitting room. There were shadows that were threatening, somehow. I can't explain it. I could show it to you."

"No," Mac said. "Mr. Thiel doesn't let people see his paintings. My father has seen one or two in New Haven, but I've never. Tell me about it."

I tried to describe it, while the rain dripped down from the leaves, tried to explain the way it had given me two feelings at once. Part of it was the place I knew, but there was something behind the light, some darkness . . . I couldn't express it satisfactorily. Mac didn't seem to notice that.

"I'm surprised he would paint it at all," he said.

"Why?" I asked. "It's the most beautiful place I've ever seen."

Mac looked at me, his eyes serious: "Don't you know? This is where his wife died. They found her at the bottom of the ravine, in the pool. They figured she'd gone over the falls. Nobody knows how she got there. She was in a coma until she died."

Chapter Seven

"*What!*" I exclaimed.

His words roared in my brain the way the wind was roaring across the sky. Everything was confusing, everything was moving about, nothing could be seen clearly because of the motion. The noise of the rain and the falls added to my confusion. It was as if, by his words, he had introduced the storm into my head itself. "Wait. Wait," I said, putting my hands over my ears.

"You didn't know," he said, when I had gathered myself together.

"I knew he was a widower," I said. "I looked at the tombstones in the cemetery. She died in '84, a few days after her father, I knew that." I felt my eyes fill with tears.

Mac looked sympathetically at me. "Did you know her?"

"How could I? I'm too young. My aunt did, they were friends. What happened?"

He shook his head. "I don't know. Nobody knows. The boys told me, at school here, and my father forbade me to gossip about it. We're outsiders here too, you know. But you must have noticed how peculiar people act about Mr. Thiel and the Callenders."

"I don't see people," I said. "Mr. Wiley at the store, but we didn't talk. Mrs. Bywall, you—you seem friendly. You don't like Mr. Callender but you like Mr. Thiel. What happened?"

Mac's face was serious. "I'll tell you what I know for facts. My father told me those so I would be clear, because some of the stories people tell—they'll say about anything, people. After old Mr. Callender moved up here and built the second house for Enoch and his family, his daughter—"

"Irene," I interrupted.

"Yes, Irene, met Mr. Thiel, somehow. I think she walked around the countryside a lot. She must have seen him painting and met him. They were married, some years later. People say he married her for her money, but that doesn't sound like something he'd do, does it?"

"I don't know. I know very little about him."

"I think he must have loved her, and she must have loved him. Because she was pretty old by then, in her thirties, and didn't believe in marriage, I bet."

"Aunt Constance never married. She says it is convenient for men, but distinctly inconvenient for women of her sort. Maybe Irene was a woman of her sort. They were friends."

"Mr. and Mrs. Thiel lived in the big house with old Mr. Callender," Mac said. "I got the feeling people liked the big house family, to an extent, even though they were strangers. Then, of course, shortly after that, Mrs. Bywall went to prison. And everybody—"

"Yes," I said. I could understand that, I could understand how local people would resent the prosecution of someone they saw as innocent because her motives were good.

"Even the big house family," Mac said. "Even though old Mr. Callender tried as hard as he could to stop his son, and everybody got to know it. Even though he hired the lawyer. There was a feeling that the Callenders had brought trouble to the town."

He thought for a minute, then went on. "Irene and Mr. Thiel had a child, and a couple of years after that— something happened, but nobody knows what—but Irene went out of the house one evening and didn't return. They searched, but in the dark, and not knowing what direction she'd gone in . . . Mr. Callender even got Enoch out to help, and they hadn't spoken for years. It was fall. The nights were long and cold. When they found her the next morning, she was unconscious. They took her home but she never regained consciousness. Old Mr. Callender had heart failure—it was the day they found her—and died. She died several days later."

There was so much I didn't understand. "Why did Irene fall? How did it happen?"

"Nobody knows."

"Was it like this? Raining? Stormy?"

"No. People wondered if she had been murdered."

"*Murdered*? Who would murder her?"

"Nobody knew, for sure. Mr. Thiel might have."

"Why?"

"He was a Hider, did you know that? And an artist. People don't trust him, he's too different. If he had married her for her money. . . ."

"Did he?"

"I don't know. How should I know? Or Enoch Callender—it's the kind of thing he'd do, I bet. But he had no motive, he was bound to inherit."

"But she was like a mother to him, she's the one who raised him really. He sounded like he really loved her."

"Or a vagrant. They scoured the country, but it would be easy to get away. If somebody tried to take her rings or her pin and she ran away. Some tramp."

"She might have just gone too near the edge and fallen."

"That's what the coroner decided," Mac said.

"What about the child?" I asked.

"Well, it was about six months later, so it was getting pretty old I guess. The nurse had quit, of course, all the local servants quit when Mrs. Thiel died. Nobody would work for Mr. Thiel. He hired a nurse, an outsider, to take care of it. They say she never left the house, they say she was a bent, wild-eyed woman in a long cape. They say she seldom spoke and had a foreign accent. They say she looked like a witch and you'd see her sometimes at night, gathering herbs, muttering to herself. They'll say anything," he told me. "Then one night, they both disappeared. The nurse and the child, both gone."

"What!" I said again. It was all incredible, there was too much of it.

"That's all anybody knows. One day, they just weren't there. Nobody has ever found out what happened. Murder? At that time it didn't seem impossible. Kidnapping?"

"What did Mr. Thiel do?"

"That's just it," Mac said, and his eyes looked away from mine, clouded briefly. "He didn't do anything. He didn't say anything. He acted as if neither Irene nor the child had ever existed. Or the nurse. If anyone said anything to him about them, he either pretended he hadn't heard or just walked away."

"What about Mr. Callender? The child would have been related to him too. Didn't he care?"

"Enoch Callender? Perhaps he did, but the villagers wouldn't speak to his family, so nobody knows."

"Because of Mrs. Bywall," I said.

Mac nodded.

"Mr. Thiel might have murdered three people," I said slowly.

"Do you think so?" Mac asked.

"It seems like a reasonable explanation," I said. "If you think carefully about it."

"Well, I don't think so," Mac said. He was reassuring me. "Your aunt has known him for a long time, hasn't she? Would she let you stay here if she thought he was a murderer?"

"Of course not," I said, smiling at the idea. "And you're right, she *would* know about it, because she would have known about his wife's death."

"You're so sensible," Mac said. "Most girls would be screaming."

"Why?" I asked, flattered. "I don't think I've taken it all in yet, that's all. I can't imagine a murderer, can you? What would make somebody so cruel? Or what might somebody want so badly that would make him take the life from another person to get it?"

Mac shook his head. "We ought to get back," he said, then added, "Or her. It could have been a woman too. Both men and women can do awful things."

"I know," I said. But I only knew from reading about it in books. I had never met anyone like that. I would not have known how to recognize evil in a person. This was something I'd never realized before. People had always been kind to me, or at least reasonably polite. Aunt

Constance, for example, and the girls at school. Even Mr. Thiel, in his dark, abrupt way. I thought then how little I knew of the world and how limited my experience was. How did I know about anybody? Even, perhaps, Aunt Constance. Although I did not seriously doubt her, it was an uneasy feeling that thought brought, and I shivered.

"We'd better go," Mac said again. "The rain's letting up. It'll be clear by tomorrow afternoon."

I felt as if it would never be clear again.

Chapter Eight

That night after dinner I went to my sitting room and, by the warm light of the kerosene lamp, reread Aunt Constance's letter. The mails took three days, so she had not received my letter when she wrote, but she had received Mr. Thiel's. Her letter told of the events of her Cambridge days, of people we both knew, of my garden, of books she had read. She remarked that Mr. Thiel seemed satisfied with my work (he hadn't bothered to say anything to me about that) and asked how the work progressed. Her letter was, like Aunt Constance herself, calm and gentle, loving. It soothed me to read it, so I did so several times, telling myself that I was trying to compose an answer to it. That was not true. I was trying to divert my mind from what Mac had told me that afternoon. I succeeded in that.

Asleep, however, my mind returned to the falls. In dreams I looked over the edge of the ravine to see somebody there, helpless, barely moving. She lifted her head to look at me and I fled, stumbling, back to my room in Mr. Thiel's house. Something had followed me there. Something, somebody, tall and dark, wrapped in a cloak, able to move soundlessly through the house. He stood beside my bed. He pulled down the bedclothes. I wept and silently begged him to go away. She was still back there in the ravine, I knew that. I wanted him to go and help her. He did not speak, but motioned with his arms to me. I was helpless. I was afraid. I did not know him. But he knew about the woman in the pool beneath the falls. The hood of his cloak hid his face in shadows.

I did as he insisted, arose from the bed. He led me down the stairs. At every step I willed my feet to turn back, to stay, to refuse to obey him. I followed him.

He opened the door of the library and motioned me in. He stepped in behind me and closed the door. The library was lit by moonlight. Each of the boxes was draped like a casket with black cloths. I tried to run but my feet would not move. The hooded figure lifted a cloth from one box and I saw that all the rug around it was damp. She was not in the ravine then, not any longer. His hand behind my head pushed me toward the box.

I could hear my heart beating. In that box, the large form, and beside it, almost cradled in its arms, another form, tiny. He had a lamp that he bought forward, the circle of yellow light approaching, to show me what was in the box. I forced my eyelids down, slowly, slowly, racing against the growing light. I could not bear to actually see. He pushed my head toward it, toward them, with one hand, his other hand on my shoulder. I screwed my eyes tight, and at last he spoke: "Open your eyes. Open your eyes. Open your eyes."

It was irresistible, that cold voice. My will swayed, my body swayed. I opened my eyes.

In the flickering light of a small lamp, I saw Mr. Thiel's face. It was his hand on my shoulder, and his face was above mine because I lay in my bed. I screamed.

I had never screamed before, and the sound frightened me. It frightened him too, I think, because he pulled back from me and his face was hidden in the shadows.

"Are you awake now?" he asked.

Then I did something else I almost never do. I burst into tears, sobbing.

"What has gotten into you?" he demanded.

I couldn't tell him, so I sobbed.

"Can't you stop that noise?" he asked. "It's no good weeping."

The door burst with light and Mrs. Bywall entered, carrying another lamp. "What is it? What's happening?" She sounded frightened.

"I dreamed—" I said, and could not finish. The darkness of my dream still lay there, behind them, waiting for me. Mrs. Bywall sat on the other side of the bed and stared at me. She looked across the bed at Mr. Thiel where he too sat waiting. "I'm sorry," I was finally able to say. "It was a nightmare."

"Well, I should think so," she said.

I noticed that both of them were in robes and night-clothes. Mrs. Bywall had braided her hair into a colorless plait. Her face showed no surprise. Mr. Thiel looked shocked and a little alarmed. "If you would fire up the stove, sir," Mrs. Bywall said, "we'll give her a glass of hot milk. It's my mother's remedy for the nightmare, and she's had many children."

"Of course," Mr. Thiel said. He left the room, relieved to be gone.

"Can you come now?" Mrs. Bywall asked. I nodded. I put on my robe and we went downstairs.

The kitchen was bright and familiar. Mrs. Bywall quickly

heated milk and poured each of us a glass. Mr. Thiel looked at his with distaste, and at the expression on his face the dark shadows of my dream left my mind.

"I'm sorry," I said. "I've woken you. I don't know what—" But I did know what.

"Tell us what it was you dreamed," Mrs. Bywall said. She looked quickly at Mr. Thiel, as if she might have spoken out of turn.

"I can't," I said.

"She was sobbing," Mr. Thiel reported to Mrs. Bywall, "and calling out."

"For Miss Wainwright," Mrs. Bywall said, nodding her head.

"No," he said shortly. "Do you often have nightmares?" he asked me. "You don't seem the type."

"Not since I was small," I told him. "Neither do I scream," I added. But somehow, remembering that, I felt an unbidden urge to smile. "I apologize for screaming at you."

"I choose to forget that," he said, but his dark eyes remembered.

"It was loud enough," Mrs. Bywall said brightly, with another glance at Mr. Thiel. "If we lived close to other people, we'd have everybody in here. It raised me up in my bed like a popover in the oven. I was that surprised." She kept looking over at my employer, as if asking permission to utter the next sentence. "You've got a good scream, Jean, loud and healthy."

At her practicality, I did smile openly, struck by the humor of what she was saying. Gradually, the ordinariness of the room entered my spirit. That sounds odd, but that's just what it felt like. It was as if the familarity of the room, of the people sitting in it with me, sipping foamy milk, as if the everyday quality of it swept the fears of my dream out of my memory. Mrs. Bywall still looked half asleep, but she talked on. I began to understand who it was she was afraid of, who it was that caused her to check and consider what she said. I began also, I thought, to glimpse the woman she really was behind her impassive face. I ignored Mr. Thiel and gave her my full attention.

"Don't I know about dreams," she said. "I had nightmares myself, before going to prison. Then, when once I was there, do you know what I dreamed of? Marlborough and my family. I had happy dreams then. I'd dream it was a birthday, when I was a child. Once I dreamed that Charlie, my Charlie, you know, came and carried me away, rescued me. I guess I never wanted to wake up from that dream."

"I don't dream now," Mr. Thiel said, entering into the conversation. "I used to. Now I paint. It may be much the same thing," he said. All during this time he watched my face closely. What did he suspect me of, I wondered; why should he watch me so closely?

"It's what you don't think of during the day that comes creeping out of your mind at night, that's what makes dreams," Mrs. Bywall said. "I can't put proper words to it, but that's what I mean."

I agreed with her theory of dreams, but did not say so. Instead I said, "It must be the middle of the night."

"Nearly so," Mr. Thiel agreed. "The wind has died down, the rain has stopped. And you have bare feet. If your aunt could see you now, she'd probably give me the rough side of her tongue."

"Yours are bare too aren't they?" I pointed out. I looked under the table. They were.

"I'm a grown man," he told me. "I'm allowed to catch my death of cold, whenever I want to. Can you sleep now?"

"I think so," I said. I remembered my manners. "Thank you for waking me."

He shrugged, as if to say that didn't matter. I returned to my room, turned down the lamp and lay quiet in the darkness. They remained downstairs. The dream did not return. Instead I found myself wondering: for whom did I call out, if not for Aunt Constance? I fell into a deep sleep before I had begun to think of an answer.

The next morning, before I started to work, I spent some time thinking carefully. I stood at one of the library windows, looking out toward the stream, over lushly grown trees. The sun was bright. The world glistened. Leaves shone in the sunlight. It was a cheerful view.

The view inside my imagination was not at all cheerful. It was gloomy and muddled, filled with vague ideas and fears. I kept my eyes on the clear world outside and thought carefully, as I had been taught.

First, my own feelings. I was, of course, embarrassed at the commotion I had caused the night before. Mr. Thiel and Mrs. Bywall had been extremely kind to me. I appreciated that, but was still embarrassed. And I understood well what Mrs. Bywall meant about things creeping out in dreams.

To learn of those deaths, those mysteries, even though they were now ten years old, frightened me. Remember, I had spent all my life under the guidance of Aunt Constance. My years, my days themselves, had been safe, secure, orderly. I knew what would come in the seasons, in the hours. Aunt Constance's patience and kindness guided me. Now, unexpectedly, I had come into a place where such deeds of darkness happened. Worse, they might have been committed by the people among whom I was living. It was as if you went to sleep in your own bed and awoke to find that same bed afloat in an endless sea, with sharks swimming about. Nothing was sure any more.

I felt that the world itself had changed and that it would never be steady under my feet again. I felt I understood nothing of people and had no way to learn. I felt fear.

Until you have felt fear, you cannot imagine it. Once you

have really felt it, you know that all your earlier nervousness was but a pale shadow. Fear that morning hung off the bottom of my heart, like a monkey with a devil's face. Its four strong hands clung at my heart, pulling down with its weight, and its hairy countenance grinned diabolically up at me with wise, dark eyes. I knew I had to look at the creature. I forced myself to do so.

I thought carefully: I *could* trust those who were not involved. I could trust Aunt Constance. I could probably trust Mac. But what of those among whom I was living? What of Mr. Thiel? What of Mrs. Bywall? And the Callenders, down the hill? All of those people were somehow concerned in this.

Aunt Constance had allowed me to come here. But could she not be deceived by this man who was so generous to her school? Whom she saw only once or twice a year? Who could so easily mislead her, by his interest—however ironic—in her ideas?

What did it all have to do with me? Why should I feel this unreasonable fear?

What had Mr. Thiel been doing in my room? Had he really heard me calling? What had he heard that brought him from his room in bare feet?

That was not careful thinking, I knew. So I started again, reassuring myself by remembering that all this had occurred ten years ago and had nothing to do with me. The death of Josiah Callender came first. Then the death of Irene Callender, Mrs. Thiel. There was the disappearance of the child and of the nurse. Those two were close together in time and probably were connected. So far, it made sense. What was the key?

Added fact: Old Mr. Callender's heart had failed him when his daughter had been brought into the house, when she had been found; although it had not failed him when she had been missing. (All of the Callenders had searched the night through, as well as Mr. Thiel.) So that old Mr. Callender must also somehow be concerned.

Arranging it in this way, like a geometry problem to be solved, eased my spirits. The answer would lie back, ten years or more, in time.

Then something struck me that should perhaps have been obvious before. There might be a clue, or the answer itself, in these boxes of papers. I thought carefully, although my imagination wanted to rush ahead. The Callenders seemed ordinary people, wealthy it was true, but even so just people, with the usual problems and quarrels, purposes and confusions. It was not usual for ordinary people to die in such fashion or to disappear. Something must have occurred those many years ago to change everything, to make these ordinary people subject to such unreasonable events.

That, also, made sense. I was an outsider, and so could not know what had happened. Mac knew, I thought, no more than he had told me, so that I could assume that the villagers also knew no more. Only the Callenders knew, and Mr. Thiel; and perhaps it was this of which Mrs. Bywall was so careful not to speak. As an outsider, I could bring no private information to the case. But I had before me seven boxes of papers, where the truth might be hidden. If so, it would most likely be in that last, half-filled box. Carefully, if I were to continue through the papers with this object in mind, I might notice something, something I would overlook in the ordinary course of things. I had organized my approach to the work, and what I was doing now was primarily tedious, just reading closely and sorting. I knew by now what to expect, so that I could work more quickly, less carefully. I could hurry through those intervening years.

I returned to the papers on the table, satisfied that I was doing all I could. Unbidden, I remembered those two tombstones and noticed something curious about Irene's. "Beloved wife of Daniel Thiel," it said, then "Beloved mother."

I wondered who had ordered those tombstones, who had caused that odd and imcomplete inscription. That information, too, might be among these papers.

At luncheon that day, Mr. Thiel asked me if I would like to accompany him to the village. I said I would not. I wanted to get back to the library, now that I knew what I was looking for. I felt hurried, as if there was some urgency to find out in time. Then, I also wanted to go back to the falls that afternoon, to see the place again as I had first seen it, to lay the ghosts of my dream.

"Have you no letter to mail?" he asked sternly. I remembered the short note I had written before going to bed the evening before. He said he would mail it for me. "Your aunt," he said, "will be concerned."

"I'll address the envelope immediately after lunch," I said. "You are kind to mail it for me."

"Mrs. Bywall and I take our responsibility for you quite seriously," he answered.

"I hadn't thought of it like that," I said, answering as tonelessly as he. "Aunt Constance believes in accepting responsibility. She makes her students be responsible to her, as well as making herself responsible for them."

"Perhaps that is one reason why her school is so successful," Mr. Thiel remarked.

"Is it successful?" I asked. I had never heard an outsider's view of Wainwright Academy. I had heard the usual complaints and gratitude, from the girls and their parents. I had noticed that everyone respected Aunt Constance.

"Don't you know? I would think you'd know that. It has the reputation, which it deserves, of giving the best education to young ladies in the Boston area. It has also the reputation of producing suffragettes, because it doesn't confine its curriculum to fine arts and domestic arts. For families who want their daughters to be educated as their sons are, it is the one place to send a female child."

"Really?" If he had meant to please me, he had succeeded.

"Really. Your aunt is a remarkable woman."

"I knew *that*," I said. "I just didn't know this. It makes me more proud of her."

He seemed willing to continue the conversation. "When I first met her the school was quite young," he said. "She has worked hard and well."

"That was before I came to her," I said carefully. *When* exactly had he met Aunt Constance, I wondered; how well did she know him?

"Oh yes, I remember," he said. As he did so, his eyes became glad, as if he had been a different kind of man in the past. "Your aunt had long been a friend of my wife's." I just nodded my head. "She was an imposing woman, your aunt. I was quite frightened when I first met her."

In my surprise I forgot that I was searching for information, and I entered into the conversation without thinking. "*You* were frightened?"

"Irene admired her. So I badly wanted her to approve of me. I was younger then." He smiled at my obvious disbelief. "And then, too, your aunt *is* such an imposing woman, so strong in her opinions, so clever in her arguments—she overwhelmed me. At first," he added, "and not for so very long, after all. She seemed to like me. Not everybody does, as you have pointed out to me," he said. "I felt sure she would be a success."

"Yes, she gives you that confidence," I agreed.

"Besides that, she introduced me to the art dealer in Boston who handles the sales of my pictures. Like many others, I am grateful to your Aunt Constance."

"I will write her more frequently," I said.

"You are very like her," Mr. Thiel said. Before I could answer, he excused himself from the table, as if he were made uncomfortable by paying me a compliment. As soon as he had left the room, my suspicions resurfaced: why should he take the trouble to make himself agreeable to me? Unless—because the papers had been in his care all these years—he knew more of what was in the boxes than he had admitted to Aunt Constance. Unless he realized that his unfriendliness might cause me to leave the house and leave the job unfinished. But why should he care about that, unless he intended me to find something he already knew was there in the boxes? Or, I thought carefully, slowly, he wanted to see if I would find something that was there to be found, unless he wanted to test the effectiveness of its concealment.

I worked for another hour after luncheon, finding nothing of interest to my particular problem. I heard Mr. Thiel leave the house. Later, I changed into my new dress and set off with bare feet to the falls. I carried a book with me, as if I planned to read. When I got there I put the book down under a tree and stood silent, to hear the sounds, to examine my own feelings. The terror the place had held in my dreams was gone. I saw that the stream was still running fast from the rains, and I approached the edge of the ravine with caution, remembering Mac's care of the day before. I lay on my stomach and looked down into the pool.

She had lain there, helpless. If you fell down the sides of the ravine, either the undergrowth or the boulders would break your fall, I thought. The sides were steep, but not sheer. The drop down, rolling as a body would, would not end at the pool of water.

If, however, you fell somehow from the falls themselves, if you were carried over the steep cliff there and tumbled down, then you would probably have broken bones. You might well be knocked unconscious.

If someone strong held you, standing where I lay, and hurled you out over the edge, down the ravine, then too you might be too injured to pull yourself out of the water.

It was just when my thoughts had reached that point that someone touched my shoulders, two strong hands. I gasped. I clutched at the ground. I tried to bury my head in the grass.

"Jean. It's only me!" Mac's voice said.

I sat up. "It is *I*," I said. "It must be nominative."

Mac looked amused. "I didn't mean to scare you."

"Where were you? Why didn't you call out that you were coming?"

"I thought you'd seen me. I've been here all along."

That was even worse.

"You were looking right at me," he protested, seeing the expression on my face. I had to believe him: his eyes were surely sincere.

"I didn't see you," I admitted.

He grinned. "You were so quiet lying here. I got worried."

"She must have either gone over the falls," I said slowly, "or have been thrown into the water."

"That's what I've thought," he said. "Unless—" he stopped.

"Unless what?" I asked.

"I don't know if I should be telling you all these things," he said. "My father got pretty mad at me last night. I told him we'd come up here. I told him I'd told you about Mr. Thiel and the nurse and all. You see," he apologized, "I'd promised him not to gossip, and so I had to tell him. But it wasn't gossiping, was it?"

"What did he say?"

"He said he thought I'd shown poor judgement. He said you were young—"

"I'm not much younger than you," I protested.

"And a girl—"

"What difference does that make!"

"He said a lot more. And then he asked me what I thought you would think of Mr. Thiel."

I could not answer that.

"He was really angry," Mac said. "And he's right."

"But it's too late, isn't it?" I argued. "You've already told me. So you might as well tell me the rest, hadn't you?"

"I don't know," Mac said. He pulled at the grass.

"Fear comes from ignorance," I said, echoing Aunt Constance. "If you're worried about frightening me, you've already done that."

"Father said that."

"And all we can do now is try to figure out what happened."

"Could we?" he asked. He looked eager. "Do you think we really could?"

"So you have to tell me. Whatever it was you thought that you weren't going to." My grammar was atrocious, but Mac understood me.

"I thought that if she had been injured somewhere else, then somebody might have brought her body up here. Maybe thinking she was dead or something."

"He'd have to be strong," I said.

"So would anyone who threw her over the edge. Otherwise," he said, "it doesn't make sense, does it? The bank is steep here, but not that steep."

I agreed with him.

"What I can't figure out is *why*," I said. "I mean, why in the first place. What difference would her death make?"

"It could have been an accident," Mac said. "That's what the jury decided it was."

"But people don't think so," I argued, "and you don't think so, and Aunt Constance didn't say so. There is something wrong."

"There was a lot of money," Mac said. "Maybe somebody wanted the money?"

"It was her father's," I said, "and he was still alive."

"It's the nurse and the child," Mac said. "That's what

makes it so very mysterious. That's what convinces me there was something wrong."

"Something dangerous."

"Something evil, I think."

For a minute I was afraid I would cry. "I don't know anything about evil," I said, feeling the helplessness I had felt in my dream take over again.

"I know some boys who would rather cheat on the exam than study for it. I know one who likes to make little kids cry, a bully. He wants them to be afraid."

"Is that evil?" I asked. "Like this is?"

He shook his head, confused. "How are we going to figure it out?" he asked.

I was glad to return to a practical question and glad to have someone to confide in. "I'm looking through the papers. I'm looking for something there, I don't know what. It would be around our age now, the child, if it lived."

He agreed. We were both, I think, thinking of what it would be like to be dead. Not even to have lived as much as we had. Or, at least, I was thinking of it.

Mac stood up, as if he couldn't sit thinking any longer. "Would you like to meet my family?" he asked, holding out a hand to pull me up. I declined his help. "I was to ask you to dinner, you and Mr. Thiel," he added. "All the rest are girls, younger than you."

"I'll ask Mr. Thiel," I said.

"I brought my Latin," he said. So we sat beneath the trees, with the sound of the falls behind us, and reviewed Latin. I enjoyed working with the precise language, after thinking so much of dark and inexplicable things.

When we returned to the house, Mr. Thiel had returned and waited for us in the library. "You've had an invitation," he said to me and gave me a letter. It had been opened, I noticed; but then I saw that it was in fact addressed to him.

"So have you," I retorted, which surprised him. I left

Mac to repeat his invitation and read the note. It was quite formal and requested the pleasure of my company for Sunday luncheon at the Callenders'. It was a woman's hand, flowing and rounded, the capitals ornate. The note had been written by Mrs. Callender. It was oddly apologetic: she excused the invitation by saying that her children did so lack companionship. Mr. Callender, his wife said, had been pleased by my cleverness and education and hoped Mr. Thiel would allow me to spend an afternoon with his children.

When I had finished reading, I looked at Mr. Thiel and he looked at me. Neither of us spoke for a minute.

"You probably want to meet the McWilliams family," he said. He was glaring at me as he said it, but I was in no mood to be cowed. Mr. Thiel added, "It is perhaps time that I begin to go out a little more."

A surprised noise burst from Mac, which he tried to turn into a cough. It was a laugh, I think. "Mother will be most pleased," he said. "She will fix a time with you." I'd never heard him speak so formally.

"What do you think?" Mr. Thiel asked Mac as he walked him to the door. "She hasn't been here more than three weeks and already there have been more invitations come into the house than in the last ten years. It all goes to show."

When he returned, however, he was not so pleasant. "So. Do you want to go there?"

I knew he did not mean the McWilliamses'. "I would like to," I said, which was an understatement: I had determined to go. "Unless you forbid me."

"I don't have that right," he said.

"I am in your charge," I reminded him. He could forbid me to go, and I would obey him. But I wanted to meet Mr. Callender's family, those graceful figures I had seen on the lawn that first day, the children of whom the father had spoken so frankly. Indeed, I wanted to see Mr. Callender again.

92

"Then I will accept for you, since the invitation was addressed to me. At least now Mrs. Bywall can have Sunday with her own family."

This was his way of reminding me, of trying to make me change my mind, but I ignored him. In fact, I went directly into the kitchen where Mrs. Bywall was beating a pot of mashed potatoes over the stove. Some of her hair had escaped. Wisps fell onto her flushed face. There was a roast in the oven and the kitchen doors were open to cool the room off.

"Mr. Thiel asked me to tell you that you might like to spend Sunday with your family," I said.

"I might indeed," she wiped her face with the apron. "But what about you?"

"I have been invited to dine at the Callenders'," I said.

"Oh," she said, and closed her lips. "I did not know you had met them."

"I met Mr. Callender in the village that day I went down," I told her.

"Have you something proper to wear?" she asked me, but her mind was elsewhere, I think. "They were more fancy down the hill, always so. You need a proper dress for the occasion." This idea seemed to upset her more than the notion of my going.

"Aunt Constance gave me a very pretty dress before I came here," I said. Mrs. Bywall insisted on seeing the dress, and although it seemed to me she barely looked at it, she pronounced that it would do wonderfully well.

I hoped it would do wonderfully well. I hoped I would do wonderfully well there too.

Chapter Nine

I dressed myself carefully for the visit to the Callenders. Something about that first scene I had spied over, where they were arrayed on the lawn, made me try to appear at my best. I could never, I knew, look elegant. But I was careful to be perfectly neat. I surveyed myself in the mirror before I went downstairs and was satisfied with the results. I had tied back my dark braids with a pink ribbon, and my image looked back at me filled with excitement. If I did not know myself, I thought, I would want to meet this lively person.

Mr. Thiel and Mrs. Bywall both awaited me at the foot of the staircase. "Don't you look nice," Mrs. Bywall said, as if she had to say something. Mr. Thiel said nothing, just stood impatiently. He insisted on driving me over in the carriage, but—even though this time I sat beside him—we had no conversation. I assumed he was angry, angry that I was going, and angry that I was eager to go. I did not attempt to speak with him. After all, why should he expect me to share his disaffections?

As we approached the Callender house, a woman came out onto the front porch, alone, to greet us. She must have been watching for us. Mr. Thiel reined in the horse and sat silent.

"Good morning, Mr. Thiel," she said, her voice so soft I could barely hear the words.

"Mrs. Callender." He inclined his head, without looking at her.

She offered me her hand and helped me down. "You are Jean Wainwright. How do you do? We are so glad you could come. Mr. Callender is detained inside, but he will be out shortly." Then she spoke to Mr. Thiel again. "He asked me to say that we will see Miss Wainwright home," she said.

Even at this Mr. Thiel did not look at her. He nodded and drove off.

Mrs. Callender must once have been pretty. Her blonde hair curled into ringlets that framed her oval face. She was slender and her carriage was straight. She should have been a lovely woman; her features were formed for smiles and cheerful conversations. Instead, she looked half-awake, as if she were speaking and moving mechanically and had not the strength to do more. Her blue eyes were faded, as if many baths in salt-water tears had bleached the color out of them. She pouted. Her hands fluttered helplessly. We stood awkwardly watching the carriage drive off. I began to wonder if my presence was unwelcome. "I hope it is not a great inconvenience to have me," I said. Mrs. Callender had taken a breath to answer when she was kept from speaking.

"On the contrary, it's a pleasure," her husband said, stepping out from the shadowed doorway just as Mr. Thiel's carriage disappeared from sight. As if he deliberately avoided meeting Mr. Thiel, I thought. He might have read my mind. "Forgive me for lurking in the background." He laughed. "We have an old quarrel, your employer and I, and we meet as little as possible. That is to say, we do not meet at all. It is odd what families will come to, isn't it? Isn't it, my dear?" He put an arm around his wife's shoulders, smiling at me. She looked at him with a kind of dumb adoration in her eyes. There was something rabbity in her face and movements, I thought.

"His wife was my sister," Mr. Callender said to me.

"I know."

"And you know about the quarrel too, I suppose?" He studied my face, his own face—for once—quiet, serious. His eyes held mine. "I'll tell you, Miss Wainwright, it's hard on a man to do what is right and then be judged so harshly for it. But in this world, you have to make choices and stand by them, regardless of what people say. And people will say just about anything, won't they?" His eyes lit with humor, and his mobile face became lively again.

I felt sympathy for him. It seemed somehow wrong that this irrepressible, good-humored gentleman should be in any way troubled in spirit.

"I'm so *glad* you could come," he said. His dark blue eyes shone with some kind of inner excitement. "There's so much to do, so much to talk about. First, you must meet the children, come along. Everyone is in the parlor, waiting. We'll make a royal progress. Priscilla?" He held out one arm for his wife and the other for me, and so we entered the house.

The parlor windows looked out over the front lawn. The room was furnished with spindly-legged tables and chairs and a large, black horsehair sofa. Over the carved wooden mantelpiece hung an oil painting of a young girl beside a younger boy. Lace doilies topped the tables. Two glass-fronted cupboards were filled with china pieces, demitasse cups, statuettes of shepherdesses and little dogs, vases and plates. All of these shone with cleanliness. A spinet piano stood in one corner, sheets of music piled on it.

The three Callender children stood in a row before the fireplace. Like their parents, they were dressed in white, the boys in white linen suits, the girl in a white dress. The oldest boy resembled his father, only somewhat dimmer, as if his features and coloring had been faded by the translation from father to son. The others resembled their mother, except in their darker hair, more brown than yellow. The girl wore her hair like her mother's, in long curls; her hands she clasped in front of her.

"My daughter, Victoria," Mr. Callender said. The girl's eyes stared into mine with no expression. Her mouth turned up in a mannerly smile.

"How do you do?" I said, wondering if I should offer to shake hands, or perhaps make a small curtsey, since she was two or three years older than I.

She inclined her head, slightly. "It's a pleasure to meet you," she said, her stiffness belying her words.

"And Joseph." Mr. Callender indicated his oldest son. This young man lounged back against the mantel and surveyed me. "If he can manage to pass the exams, he will go into Harvard next year, or Yale. If not . . ."

"There is always the army," Joseph drawled. "Or the merchant marine. One would prefer those, don't you know." He smiled lazily at me as he spoke, ignoring the quick disapproving frown on his father's face. He didn't look as if he would prefer an active life, but I knew better than to judge from appearances alone.

"How do you do," I said.

"You'll disappoint Miss Wainwright," Mr. Callender told him. "She has her mind set on an education."

"*Chacun á son goût*," Joseph remarked.

"And Benjamin." He stepped forward and shook my

97

hand clumsily. Then he stood back into line, watching his father.

It was an uncomfortable moment. At a word from Mr. Callender, we all sat down, around the room. Mr. Callender looked from one to the other of us. "Aren't first meetings awful," he remarked, but he looked as if he was enjoying himself.

"Father has told us so much about you," Joseph said to me.

"You're quite superior, we've been told," Victoria added. She sat with the perfectly straight back of a young lady, her skirts smooth over her legs; she looked at her older brother, not at me, as she spoke.

"My husband tells us you live in Boston," Mrs. Callender said, her voice so soft I could barely hear her.

"Yes," I said.

"Don't you find Marlborough dull?" Victoria asked. Just as I opened my mouth to answer she went on. "I do. If I lived in Boston I wouldn't care to spend a summer here. But then, I'm not a superior person."

"She's employed," Benjamin told her. He had his feet on the rungs of his chair and he shifted restlessly in his seat. "Rooting about among Grandfather's papers. Finding out all of our secrets." He at least looked at me, a rather sidelong glance that seemed to me not friendly. I thought I understood then what might have caused the hostility of these young Callenders that had puzzled me.

"I haven't found out any secrets," I reassured them. "Just dinner menus and lists of linens, a few notes accepting or declining invitations. Although there is the correspondence between your grandfather and his father."

"Isn't that an odd occupation for a young lady, father?" Victoria asked.

"I wouldn't mind any occupation," Benjamin remarked.

"It's not exactly fine stitching or watercoloring." Joseph agreed with Victoria.

I answered Benjamin, since Mr. Callender seemed content to sit back and listen. "I agree with you. I have been employed, one way or another, almost as long as I can remember. My aunt, with whom I live, has a school, and there is always something useful to do."

"That's not what I meant," Benjamin told me impatiently.

"Benjamin," his father warned him.

"Well, it isn't."

"Then what did you mean?" I asked. He reminded me, with his truculence, of some of the younger girls at the school, trying to pick a quarrel so that they would have attention.

"Nothing," he said.

"Benjamin," Joseph drawled at me, "thinks he is the reincarnation of our great-grandfather."

"More than you at least," Benjamin answered quickly. "There's nothing wrong with wanting that."

"Why do you hope that?" I asked, because I had not liked the sound of the elder Enoch Callender in his letters, and I wondered if he was more admirable than he had seemed.

"He got what he wanted," the boy said. "Nobody stood in his way for long. He always got what he wanted."

"What is it that you want?" I asked him. He had spoken so intensely that I was curious to know what could move him so.

"Money," he answered promptly. "Money and more money."

"Everybody knows that, you donkey," Victoria said.

"The question is how," Joseph said. "What great-grandfather was good at was knowing how to make it.

When he was your age, he was already a rising young man."

"I can't help that," Benjamin said. "At least I'm not sitting back and waiting to marry it."

Joseph laughed easily, which didn't help Benjamin's temper. Mr. Callender caught my eye and smiled at me, as if he and I were above this sort of talk but were indulging the children.

"We have little to do but daydream," he said to me. "Victoria has declared her intention of marrying a prince. But she has not yet decided whether he should be Italian or French."

Victoria flushed and raised her chin. "Well, I would," she said. "Once we leave here, there's no reason why I shouldn't. Unless I'm too old."

"If I had a ship, just one," Benjamin said, "there are fortunes to be made, selling guns or transporting labor— like the Chinese; there are millions of them and they'll pay to be brought to California. You can carry thousands and just offload them. Then I'd buy arms and sell them in the Orient, on my way to pick up another cargo of Chinese."

"Ships go down," Joseph pointed out.

"Not mine."

"You think you're so realistic, but you're just like the rest of us," Victoria told him.

Benjamin squirmed in his chair, but looked stubbornly at his sister.

Mrs. Callender had been gazing absently out the window, but now she rose. "If you'll excuse me, I must go to the kitchen. Victoria?"

"Mother," Victoria protested, with a gesture of her hand that included her dress, and me. Mrs. Callender waited patiently. "If you insist," Victoria said, rising from her seat, with visible reluctance.

"We have no servants," Mr. Callender told me. "We live quite modestly."

I changed the subject. "That is an interesting portrait." I looked at the painting above the mantel. It was not, really, but I didn't want Mr. Callender to feel the need to apologize to me.

"Do you think so? It's a relic of happier days."

I looked at it carefully. The two children stood side by side on an oriental rug, stiff as mannequins. Their eyes stared out at me. The youngest, the boy, was four or five; the girl nearer my own age. The boy was the center of the picture, his halo of golden curls surrounding his round face, his expression angelic. He wore velvet and lace; his mouth turned up at the corners; his skin glowed pink and white. As if she were in the portrait to emphasize the beauty of the boy, the girl was in shadows, dark-haired and plain. She too wore velvet and lace, but her face looked serious and her eyes held a hint of sadess.

"You can guess who they are," Mr. Callender said.

"You and your sister?"

"Yes. We had nurses, of course, but it was Irene who took care of me. She dedicated her life to me, I'm afraid; and that kept her from marrying at a proper age. I worried about that, I urged her to go out and meet people. But she said she preferred not. We never expected her to marry, my father and I. When I married, I thought she would always live with us, that we might be her family. I know Priscilla hoped the same. I thought we might repay her earlier sacrifices."

"You must have been happy when she did marry," I remarked, still looking at the portrait. This girl had become the wife of Mr. Thiel, *beloved wife*, I remembered.

"Why of course." He paused. "I wished her all happiness, of course. We saw her much less frequently after she married. I don't think Joseph remembers her at all, and certainly not Benjamin nor Victoria. You ought to tell Miss Wainwright about your studies, Joseph."

"She wouldn't be interested," he said.

"But I would be. I'm very interested in education," I said.

"Ah, yes. Yes, I can see you would be. I'm studying the usual thing, don't you know."

I bit back the sharp rejoinder that was on my tongue. "Do you study with your brother?" I asked Benjamin.

"Who needs to know that stuff?" he asked me, angry. "Only gentlemen."

"Like it or not, you are a gentleman," his father reminded him. Benjamin looked angrily at me, as if that were somehow my fault. Joseph laughed again. "Although you have lamentable tendencies toward the barbarian," Mr. Callender continued.

"Joseph has studied some Greek," Mr. Callender said, addressing me.

"Who teaches you?" I asked him.

"Father," he told me.

"We have a schoolroom. I don't want my children to be disadvantaged by their years of seclusion here," Mr. Callender told me. "So that I temporarily put on my Platonic garb, training up these young Alexanders."

"You speak as if you will be moving away."

"In time, inevitably," Mr. Callender said.

"Where to?" I asked.

"That we are not sure of. The ladies prefer Newport, at least for the summers, and London or Paris for the other seasons. Joseph doesn't really care where we live as long as there will be stables. That's correct, isn't it?"

"And a hunting season," Joseph added. "London would be the best choice, if you ask me. Benjamin would conduct his commercial life—whatever that was—and you would have a club, and Victoria would have the season there. The climate is unpleasant, I've heard, but the theater and opera would compensate. The stores are fashionable, the houses pleasant, the society lively."

When he spoke like that, he sounded interested in his topic. "You have thought it all out," I observed.

"We have time to dream here," Mr. Callender answered me. "We're great dreamers, aren't we? Even Benjamin. And yet I can't condemn us, because I don't think there's any great enterprise that didn't begin as somebody's dream. What do you dream of, Miss Wainwright?"

"I? Why nothing really," I told him.

"Not even your studies? Your ambitions?"

"Those aren't dreams," I said. "They're plans."

"So are mine," Benjamin declared.

Looking at it from a different angle, I could understand what he meant.

Mr. Callender voiced my objection. "Except yours have all to do with money."

"What could be more practical?" Joseph asked. "That's true, isn't it, Miss Wainwright?"

"Money is certainly practical," I agreed.

"You sound unsure," Mr. Callender said.

"Perhaps because I can't imagine the riches you are thinking of," I admitted.

"We must cultivate your imagination," he said. "And you will cultivate our common sense. It should prove an admirable exchange."

"Perhaps little Miss Wainwright doesn't care to have her imagination cultivated," Joseph said.

"Perhaps you do not care to be realistic," his father answered sharply.

Victoria summoned us to the table then, and I was grateful for the interruption. Mr. Callender gave me his arm to enter the dining room and smiled down at me as we crossed the hallway, his whole face alight. I could not resist smiling back.

The long table was set with linens and silver. Glass goblets filled with chilled water stood at each place. Mrs. Callender had prepared a formal meal. We seated ourselves, and she hurried out from the kitchen bringing plates of muddy soup. Victoria helped her to clear the first course and bring in the main dishes. Mr. Callender carved the roast at a sideboard while Victoria passed china bowls of mashed potatoes, creamed spinach, a gravy boat and silver trays where rolls lay in white napkins. Mrs. Callender was apparently no cook. The soup was tasteless, the rolls yeasty, the meat tough and the potatoes lumpy. For dessert she brought out a lopsided cake. I cleaned my plate, as I had been taught, but declined seconds. Benjamin ate vigorously, I noticed, and Joseph had a good appetite. Mr. Callender ate little, less than his wife and daughter. Afterward, I asked if I could help with the washingup. Mr. Callender protested, but I insisted.

"You have taken a great deal of trouble for me," I said to my hostess as I tied an apron over my dress. The kitchen was crammed with dishes and pans. "Thank you so much for the dinner," I said.

Mrs. Callender was carefully washing the goblets, as if afraid she might break one. She did not look up at me, so deep was her concentration on the task. I took a towel to dry them with. "It wasn't very good," she said. "I never learned, you see. I wasn't taught. It wasn't expected that I would need actually to keep house. But Mr. Callender wanted everything at its best for you."

"Oh dear," I said. "I don't know where he got an idea like that."

"He has his ideas," she said. "There is so much he wants . . . and he was so disappointed in the meal."

"Surely not," I protested.

"You don't know him well. I do. He has such high standards." It seemed to me that she might weep. "He is a disappointed man," she said, and the tears began to flow. Her hands continued with the washing. "I am a disappointment to him. The children too."

"Don't cry, Mrs. Callender," I said. I was embarrassed for her and for myself.

"You won't tell him I said so?" she asked suddenly, her eyes meeting mine then shying away. "We mustn't talk like this. You won't tell him?"

Thinking how much she must care for him, to care so deeply about his disappointments, to want to protect him from worry, I made the promise warmly.

At that she smiled timidly at me. "You seem like a nice child," she said. "Maybe it will all turn out for the best." All what? I wondered, as she went on. "Do you know what *my* dream is? I would hire a housekeeper and a staff of servants. He could live in New York, in a home that would be pleasant for him; he always preferred New York to any city. The children too. I might go there. Or I might go to be a missionary, somewhere. There is so much good that needs to be done. A quiet life. And I don't care what I wear, or what I eat. He does. They do."

I could think of nothing to say. Quite suddenly her expression became sharp and her voice changed. "Someday it will all happen as we wish it, what do you think?" She laughed, a high, nervous sound. "Until then, Mr. Callender says we must think of this as a life of charming rusticity. It's only a matter of time, only waiting." She looked at me out of the corner of her eye. "There was a French queen who played at being a shepherdess, Mr. Callender says. Do you think Joseph is a handsome boy?"

I answered as I knew she wanted me to: "Very."

"He'll break hearts, won't he? Will he break your heart?"

"I hope not," I said.

"You're too young to know yet. He's like his father at that age. He hasn't had much chance to socialize here. There is nobody here who is his equal, unfortunately. We must live in isolation for now. But if we can leave here before it is too late, Joseph will do well. I will pin my hopes on Joseph. He can be delightful, you know. He dances gracefully too; we have taught him the accomplishments of a gentleman. Benjamin is too young, I think. You will like Joseph."

When at last we finished, we went through the dining room and back out to the parlor. There Victoria sat at the piano, her back straight, her wrists arched. Her father and brothers stood behind her and they were singing a song from *HMS Pinafore*, "The Admiral Song." Mr. Callender sang the part of the admiral, comically, with exaggerated expression, strutting around the room. His children joined in on the harmony at the chorus. Mrs. Callender and I sat to listen, enjoying the performance. Led by Mr. Callender, his children were more lively and happy than I had thought they could be. After they finished that song, Mr. Callender asked Victoria to sing "Buttercup," which she did in a sweet true voice, accompanying herself.

"Do you sing, Miss Wainwright?" Mr. Callender asked me.

His three children looked at me as if they had forgotten my presence. A silence awaited my answer. "No," I said, which was the truth. I do not sing well. "Neither do I dance."

"But almost anybody can learn to sing," he said. "And everybody can learn to dance. Isn't that true? We'll have to take your education in hand, won't we, children? Would you let us do that, Miss Wainwright?"

"I think I would be grateful," I told him.

"Your wonderful aunt is too busy for such frivolous endeavors?" he asked me.

"She is certainly fully occupied," I said. "She has many responsibilities." I did not want him to think I would speak slightingly of Aunt Constance.

"She must be an entirely admirable woman," he answered quickly. "But now have we time for a game of croquet before I return you to Mr. Thiel's house?" He glanced at his pocket watch. "No, just to set up the game. I'll walk you to the ford, which will be quicker than going through the village, if that is all right with you?" His eyes glowed as if he were afraid I would forget that the bridge across the falls was a secret.

"That's half a mile beyond the falls," Victoria said. She turned around on the piano stool to look at me. "You must be a strong walker," she said sweetly, her voice hinting that there was something unladylike about that accomplishment.

"I am," I said, and did not pretend to apologize for it.

"If we had a carriage, we could return you in proper style," Victoria said, to no one in particular.

"If wishes were horses, beggars would ride," Joseph said to her.

"Let's *play*," Benjamin urged.

Mr. Callender led us outside to the green lawn and thus I became, temporarily, a part of that group of figures I had seen weeks earlier. Mrs. Callender sat in a lawn chair, her parasol shading her face. Mr. Callender and I watched the start of the game. Benjamin led off with a quick stroke that put his ball too far into the center of the court. Victoria followed with a weaker shot that left her ball where Joseph could lazily just nudge it with his and then send it sideways off the court in a penalty shot. They paid no attention to Mr. Callender and me, and we walked away without farewells.

When we were well out of earshot Mr. Callender spoke. "How did you like us?" he asked. "And my Joseph, how did you like him? You see now why I think he needs someone like yourself, with purpose and direction. Someone like yourself would bring out the best in him, and we all need that, don't we? Someone to bring out the best in us. You were kind to help Mrs. Callender with the washing-up. I'm afraid Victoria isn't the most willing assistant—she prefers more decorative poses. I appreciate your thoughtfulness."

I didn't say anything. I was wondering why both Mr. and Mrs. Callender kept talking to me about Joseph, as if I were of marrying age. I walked ahead of Mr. Callender, up a narrow path through the trees that crowded up this side of the little river. His voice came from behind me, "People say that silence is golden. I quarrel with that. Silence is secretive and you wonder what the other person is thinking. I see the curve of your neck and hear your footsteps, but I ask myself—what is she thinking? Her one braid gives no clue. If only the braid could speak. Braid, speak to me."

I smiled back at him over my shoulder, amused.

"My children have taken quite a liking to you."

"They have?" I asked, betraying surprise.

His hand on my shoulder stopped me, and he moved up to stand beside me. "We don't have the graces you are accustomed to, Miss Jean Wainwright. My children are more awkward than they might be, they lack polish, they lack learning. I thought you would have the perception to see that. There is little gaiety in their lives—you will have realized that—little occasion for them to learn proper behavior."

"You do seem isolated." More isolated, in fact, than Mr. Thiel. "I spoke thoughtlessly," I apologized, and I was sincere in that. The severity left his face as quickly as it had arrived there. It was right, I thought, that he should speak shortly to me for my failure to think carefully about his children, about the difficulties of their life.

"I do like your lack of pride," he said as we walked side by side. "May I pay you a compliment? It always seems to me that such open-mindedness is a sign of a truly rational character. And you lead me to be more open-minded too, because I have to own that my children's behavior was not perfect. I can excuse them if you can, but I will remember that they could have been more welcoming. After all, good manners don't depend entirely on gracious living, do they? Maybe even, I excuse them more than I should because they are the victims of the adult world. It is for no fault of their own that they live here, live so; yet because they are children, they are helpless."

I had often thought just that about the girls at the Wainwright Academy, when I had seen how they were molded by the errors and even the vices of their parents. I agreed with Mr. Callender. "It's my fault," he acknowledged. "You've met my wife now, you see how she is, so the responsibilty rests on my shoulders." He looked at his shoulders, as if measuring them. "You'll be a good influence on me, young as you are. A man should always seek out good influences on himself, don't you think? Gather them to him. It would be better if we could leave here."

"Why can't you?"

"The Callender fortune is here," Mr. Callender said. "Inacessible at this time, except for enough"—he pinched his fingers together—"just enough to live on. There is"—he hesitated—"a will. A huge, labyrinthine will, cased in iron and silent as the grave that holds its maker. Like a mausoleum, I sometimes think, with wrought iron gates and a key so heavy it breaks the neck of whomever carries it, just by its weight."

"Surely it can't be so intricate," I said, trying to disguise my amusement at his way of overstatement, at the extravagant picture his imagination drew. If I was going to be a good influence, I knew I ought not to encourage this extravagance.

"No, of course not, but it is less depressing to think of it so. I try to avoid depression, in all things. There is so much to sorrow and worry me—it's not even the children or Priscilla's quiet unhappiness." He looked at me, and I was glad to see that he understood his wife. "Not even that hydra-headed will. You see, when my sister was lost to me"—he held my eye—"her child was also lost." I wondered how the loss of the young child could matter so much, even to an uncle, after so long a time. But I did not wonder aloud, because the sincerity of his feeling was evident in his face. "The worst of it is that in the child's disappearance there is an unsolved mystery. *That* is what is so hard to bear. You're wise enough to have noticed that about life I think. My sister is dead, there is no mystery in that. I saw her buried. That is grief to me, but it is a fact. For her child, there is no such surety. The child's own father will not speak of the matter. Almost as if . . ." his voice trailed off, but I understood what he did not say. He went on quickly, as if to distract me, as if he had just recalled in whose house I was living. "If I knew my sister's child were dead, it would be easier for me to bear, much easier than this insoluble mystery. Does that sound selfish?"

"Not really, no. I think I can understand," I said.

"But it is selfish, in its way. It wouldn't do for you and me not to be honest with one another, I want to be careful of that in itself. But when I think of children, my own as well as others, and what the world is like even for my own, who have at least a solid roof and regular meals. The poor creature—my sister's child—might be anywhere, living under who knows what circumstances."

I felt pity for him, and admiration too. He carried this sorrow in his heart, but didn't inflict it on others.

"So you see me as I am," he said, his voice briefly

solemn, before it switched again to contain an undercurrent of humor, "such as I am. There are so many things I could do here. I can read your mind a little, and I too regret that I lack the power of character to occupy myself usefully. I could study, even become a scholar. Or farm. I could write novels in the long mornings; my imagination is certainly up to that I think, don't you?"

Laughing, I agreed.

"Or at least memorize the names of all the kings of England, starting with Ethelred. I could do something— learn card tricks?—instead of letting old wounds trouble me, make me gloomy . . ." His voice trailed off, wistfully, it seemed.

"Are you gloomy now?" I wondered. He was a hard person to understand, I thought, more mercurial in his nature than anyone I'd ever met.

"How could I be, in such good company, on such a temperate afternoon?"

"I don't know," I told him. "But are you?"

We were at the falls by then and he stopped so I could look at him. "You tell me, Miss Jean Wainwright. You tell me and I will believe you."

I studied him, his bright, open countenance, the brightness of his golden head and white suit. "I don't know," I told him honestly. "I can't imagine it, but I don't have much imagination."

"Then you'll have to get to know me better. You'll enjoy that—I flatter myself. I know *I* will, because you will come back to see us again, won't you? Next week?"

I hesitated, thinking of that unhappy family and the brave appearance they put on for my sake.

"You did enjoy yourself, just a little, didn't you?" he asked me.

"Yes I did, but you will have to promise me something."

"Anything," he declared extravagantly, his hand over his heart.

"Mrs. Callender worked so hard, that was clear, and I think you eat more simply when you are not entertaining. Will you promise me not to treat me as a guest, that she will go to no extra trouble for me?"

Mr. Callender looked deeply into my eyes. "Such a thoughtful young lady," he said. "How fortunate for us. I make the promise gladly, and gratefully too."

He lowered the board down over the falls and gestured me onto it with a bow like that Raleigh must have used when he laid his jeweled cape over a puddle for his sovereign queen. I did not let him see how frightened I was of crossing the steep falls on that narrow board. I stepped over with what I hoped was convincing confidence. It had, of course, occurred to me that this secret bridge might explain Irene Callender Thiel's otherwise inexplicable fall.

Chapter Ten

It was in the late afternoon when I got back to Mr. Thiel's house. I found my employer in the kitchen preparing a dinner. A fowl roasted in the oven, potatoes boiled in a pan on the stove. He was shelling peas.

"So you're back," he said, looking at me briefly, sharply. "You can set the table. We'll eat in here." His hands were deft, splitting the pods open and letting the peas fall into a stoneware bowl. "I thought you'd be hungry."

"I am," I said. I had not eaten much at the lunch, despite having cleaned my plate. The servings were small at the Callender house.

"Young McWilliams brought us a pheasant," Mr. Thiel said.

"Where is Mrs. Bywall?"

"She'll return after dark," he said. "She likes to stay as long as she can with her family."

The meal tasted good to me. In fact, it was delicious. "You cook well," I said, partly to thank him, partly because I was surprised.

"I lived alone for many years and taught myself to cook. It isn't hard."

"Why do you employ Mrs. Bywall?"

"The house must be kept as well," he reminded me. "How did you find the Callenders? Did you enjoy yourself?"

"They have invited me to return next Sunday," I said, not answering either of his questions.

"What did you say to that?"

"I accepted."

He nodded.

"They went to a great deal of trouble for me," I explained. Somehow, he made me feel that I should not have accepted.

"Enoch Callender has ambitions," Mr. Thiel answered. "His wife—has trouble meeting his notions of what is necessary in life."

"She has no help," I defended her.

"The villagers have long memories. It's her own fault, as I see it. They made their beds."

"Was it only because of Mrs. Bywall?" I asked. "Mr. Callender said he had little money, and I think they can't afford servants. They are very unhappy, I think."

"Do you," he said coldly.

"Yes, I do." I was a little angry. "They can't seem to manage housework well, and yet they dress so beautifully, just for themselves. They have no friends. You, at least, have some friends."

"So they're even worse off than I am," he said. He uttered a harsh laugh. "They seem to have made a friend of you."

I didn't contradict him, although I could have. After all, I did like Mr. Callender. He spoke to me as if I were an adult, and he listened to me when I spoke. "Mr. and Mrs. Callender were accustomed to a more social life, weren't they? In New York? Something gayer, more civilized, more exciting. It's clear they've lost a great deal. Yes, I sympathize with them."

"So I see," Mr. Thiel said. He wold have liked to drop the subject, I could tell that. But I continued. "Did Mr. Callender's father deny him his inheritance?" I asked. "Is that what happened? Mr. Callender doesn't speak respectfully of his father. Was it because of Mrs. Bywall?"

Mr. Thiel looked angry, but he answered me. "Mrs. Bywall was only the last straw. But those two never got along. They never would have. They were two different kinds of people. Josiah preferred his daughter to his son."

"Why?" I asked. For a minute, I thought he would refuse to answer me, but at last he did, speaking unemotionally.

"Josiah and his daughter shared concerns, for education and better living conditions for working people. They fought the injustice of the world whenever they could. Enoch was different; even as a child he was different, Irene said. She blamed herself, but I always thought he would have been as he was even if he had been raised differently. He got everything he wanted, but nothing satisfied him, there was never enough for him. And he didn't care about learning or law or people. He cared only about pleasure, his own pleasure, and his own comfort. Many young men do, and like many young men he gambled, he was in debt, he purchased on credit and did not pay his bills. He not only had no concern for the things his father and sister cared about, he also never missed a chance to quarrel with them.

"His sister, my wife, loved him, she always loved him. It was a failing in her, a blind spot. She said he was different from the rest of the world and should not be treated in the same way. She said he was a wild thing, not to be tamed, not to be thought of as good or bad. She indulged all his whims and yet more often than not he made her weep. Sometimes he made her angry. But she did love him. His father—couldn't. Josiah felt guilty about that, of course, so Enoch could often get his own way with his father as well as Irene. Enoch tried to talk Josiah out of selling the factory and moving here. In that, at least, his father was firm. At first, Enoch simply refused to move out here, but Josiah forced him to.

"They hoped that when he married he would settle down. His wife brought him some money, but that didn't last long. So he had to move here and he resented it. He said he was wasting himself here and quarreled constantly with his father. He never let up, always asking to return to the city, never missing an opportunity to denigrate his father's hopes, choices. When I married his sister—well, he has never liked me. To answer your question then, no, I don't think Mrs. Bywall was to blame. The years before, if anything, were to blame. Yes, Josiah cut him out of the will, unless there was no one else. Enoch does have a generous allowance. But nothing will ever be enough for him, unless he has everything. There are many people like that."

I thought about this, and how strongly Mr. Thiel apparently felt about Mr. Callender. I had never heard him make such a speech before, not even in his arguments with Aunt Constance.

"Did *you* inherit the fortune?" I asked.

"That is impertinent," he said. He was right, and I apologized.

Still, I had more questions. I didn't know how long Mr. Thiel would continue the conversation. He did not look at me as he spoke, and his voice was cold; but he did continue speaking. So I persisted. "If Mr. Callender didn't like his son, couldn't he have tried to change him?"

Mr. Thiel sighed patiently and explained in the voice of a

teacher talking to a rather dull child: "He did try. He didn't succeed. Irene was the only one who could talk sense to her brother, and even she couldn't talk him into being what he did not want to be. Maybe she loved him too much. She tried to protect him from his father. She tried to protect his father from him. She tried to bring the two together. There was nothing she could do, but she wouldn't admit that."

I considered all of this. Then I said, "If you look at it from his point of view, there is much to pity him for. Mr. Callender, that is."

Then Mr. Thiel did look at me with his steady dark eyes. His eyes seemed to probe into my mind. It was uncomfortable. "Of course," he said, "that is true. However, if you believe that, then you must also believe that there is no importance to the question of right and wrong." I understood what he was driving at. But he went on as if I needed to have things more clearly explained. "If you believe that you must also think that there is not Truth, beyond all of us human creatures."

"Do you mean God?"

"No, I mean something human. God is in the realm of good and evil. Truth, the simple truth, the clear truth—*that* is for human beings."

"I don't understand," I said.

"I mean," he spoke carefully and even more slowly, "that if, for example, you feel sympathy for Mr. Callender because of what he has lost, as he sees it; if you take his point of view about things; if it is a right thing for Enoch to want to spend money for his own transient pleasures rather than for schools for poor children; then, you could have such a sympathy for everyone, in every situation, couldn't you? And then everyone could be excused for anything, however cruel or destructive it is."

I understood what he meant. "But you felt sympathy for

Mrs. Bywall," I argued. "You saw things from her point of view."

"That was different," he said.

"Why?" I insisted. "She stole, didn't she? That's not right."

"She didn't lie about what she'd done," Mr. Thiel said. "She accepted her punishment."

Reluctantly, I found myself switching sides: "And she did it for the good of somebody else, there is that, too."

Mr. Thiel thought about that. "No, that can't be a good excuse, can it? Anybody could say they were doing a good deed for the sake of somebody else. John Wilkes Booth shot Mr. Lincoln for the sake of freedom for all men, he said."

"You think that the whole difference is in telling the truth," I said slowly, thinking aloud now. "Did Mr. Callender lie?"

Mr. Thiel didn't answer this question. Instead he said, "The important thing is to find the truth. To be honest with yourself. Take slavery. Say a man has always owned slaves and always believed that they were not humans. So he treats a slave as if he were a cow or chicken, buys and sells, disciplines, even slaughters sometimes. You could understand how that slave owner felt and how he came to believe what he believed, couldn't you?" I nodded. He continued, "But there is another man, a black man, equally a man. If you sympathize with the slave owner, you must accept slavery itself. Unless the most important thing is the truth."

"But you wouldn't go to war, you were a Hider," I protested. I thought I had gone too far, but after a long moment he did answer me.

"Any use I have in the world is in these—" he held out his hands. "So yes, I did do that, I ran away. Had my family been able to buy my way out as Josiah Callender's father did for him, I'd have done that instead. I would *not* risk my own death, not until I had painted. It was a miserable life I led, except for the painting. Most people despised me. They were right in that. I despised myself. I would do the same thing again, however."

"Would you despise yourself again?"

"Yes, that too."

That did not make sense to me. It seemed, from the way he described his choices, that there was no right decision Mr. Thiel could make. That confused me, because I was accustomed to the solutions arrived at by careful thought; but in this discussion, careful thought led me further from the solution. Mr. Thiel sat and watched me and said no more. I wondered why he had allowed the conversation to go on as long as it had. I did not flatter myself that he was growing interested in my character, so I wondered what his purpose was in talking with me.

The next few weeks passed quietly. I worked every morning, studied with Mac in the afternoons, or explored the woods with him. Sometimes I helped Mrs. Bywall in the garden. I wrote letters to Aunt Constance and received letters from her. I told her everything, everything except my curiosity about the death of Mrs. Thiel and my determination to see if the papers held a clue to that mystery. It was not that I wanted to keep it a secret from her. No, I just wanted to spare her the pain that the memory would bring. I simply did not mention my thoughts about the chain of events of earlier years.

Every Sunday I was taken to luncheon at the Callenders. I saw little of the children of the house, and it was soon apparent that I was Mr. Callender's guest. Mrs. Callender never again spoke to me as she had that first time. She seldom spoke at all. The two boys and their sister managed not often to be present either before the meal or after, so that as a rule we were together only for the meal itself. Mr. Callender still insisted that they had an unusual fondness for me, but I could not agree. However, since the idea seemed to please him and there was no good to be accomplished by disabusing him, I did not point out the truth. Then, after washing up with Mrs. Callender and Victoria, who always joined us after that first week, I would walk with Mr. Callender. Those were the best parts of the afternoon.

He must have had a wild streak as a young man. He could talk about gambling houses and the dockside area of New York in a way that brought them alive before me. I would never know those worlds for myself, but he enabled me to see into them, for a brief while. He made me understand what is called the "Underside of Life," a world inhabited by ne'er-do-wells and actresses, by men and women who live a secret nighttime life. These were bold characters, some of them, with a lack of concern for their own safety, a love of the dramatic and daring and a disregard for the tenets of society. Others he spoke of were ruined by drink or addiction to gambling, and to worse things I gathered, but he only hinted at those. The society he described had its own aristocracy, as well as peasantry. He spoke of casinos, lit by crystal chandeliers and attended by handsome men with beautiful, bejeweled women on their arms. He spoke of the excitement of the cards, of men made rich or ruined by a turn of a wheel. He spoke of cutthroats, pickpockets, burglars and sharpers. "These desperate people commit illegal crimes," he said. "And on the whole I prefer them to those who commit legal crimes, the moneylenders, the men who manipulate paper fortunes or who have lawyers to find out loopholes in the laws. These criminals I speak of risk it all," he said, "and do not talk hypocritically about respectability. I'm a romantic, I know you're thinking that, but you mustn't let your own rightness blind you to the rightness of others." And he put his hands over his eyes, stumbling comically, to illustrate his point.

But Enoch Callender was also well acquainted with

respectable life in New York and could talk of balls and teas, of summer homes in Watch Hill and Newport. Sometimes he made mock of the respectable people, but he made them vivid, too; the old women sitting and watching each other like jealous monarchs, the debutantes and their esquires, the yacht racing and lawn tennis, operas and plays.

Once, to my confusion, he insisted on teaching me to waltz. He said every young lady should know how to dance properly and would not attend me when I pointed out that dancing and balls could have little place in my life. He showed me the steps and then, singing the melody, held out his hands to me. It was as if he had read my secret wishes. We danced around and around the grassy dell. Gradually, I sang the tune with him and felt my legs, as they became accustomed to the steps, grow more confident, more quick. At last, dizzy, we stopped, and he gravely clapped his palms softly together, as if we had been at a ball. I laughed and did the same.

"You have a light foot, Jean," he said to me. I knew, but did not say so because I was still out of breath, that I danced well because he led me well, just as in singing there are some voices with which your own sounds truer, stronger. "You take me back to my youth," he said. "Oh, there were balls I have danced at—with nobody more appealing than my present partner, I must own it—but let me tell you what it was like then."

He showed me worlds I would never inhabit. But after speaking with him, I knew more than I could have learned myself by living in them. His words stirred my imagination. They made me understand how large and various the world outside Cambridge was. "Don't you want to see it, Jean?" he would exclaim. "Don't you want to be out there? You can admit it to me, you can be sure I'll understand."

"No," I said. "No, I don't think so. But I enjoy hearing about it from you."

"Why don't you want to live it yourself?"

"It would not suit me," I said, I think correctly. "I am not at my best at gaiety. I am at my best in a sedate life. When things happen too quickly—"

He shook his head and smiled at me with satisfaction. "You underestimate yourself, I suspect. I am willing to take your good opinion of Aunt Constance, that famous woman, but I don't believe she appreciates the whole of you. You must not let yourself become too respectable. Keep yourself a little wild. What is life for, if not for the living of it?"

His enthusiasm was contagious, and he could see it in my face. "Wouldn't you like to see the world? Japan," he said, "Tahiti, Rome, Kashmir, Madagascar."

"Of course," I said. This did not seem to me related to what had gone before. "But one cannot do everything, one cannot have everything."

"Why not?" he asked with a laugh. "And even so, even if it is so, why shouldn't the imagination want everything?"

I enjoyed those times. My own tongue was loosened, and although he listened to what I said, he did not always take my words seriously, so that I came, myself, to take them less seriously. But somehow, I never spoke to him about his own family, and I never mentioned the unhappy events of ten years ago, thoughts of which occupied so much of the rest of my time. He occasionally mentioned his father, bitter references. His sister he seldom spoke of, as if it were too painful for him to do so. I did not want to increase his burden of sorrow by bringing up my own questions.

Yes, I liked Mr. Callender. He was so many things— quick and experienced, a man of adventures who knew strange and sometimes unsavory places and could make those places live in my imagination. It was exciting to be with him. He had, besides, a grace of his own. None of his gestures were awkward. He seemed a Renaissance man, able to do everything well and widely informed. Despite this, he did not make me feel awkward or clumsy or childish, as he so easily might have. He made me feel as graceful as himself, as rich in imagination, by including me in his memories, by talking with me so naturally. In his presence, I became more clever, less stiff and childishly ill at ease, as if some of his worldly charm could rub off and become part of my own being. And yet it was not a shallow friendship, I thought. I understood that a deep sorrow lay beneath his gaiety, and I admired the gallantry with which he went on with his life.

Mr. Callender made me joyful. I looked forward eagerly to our meetings.

I was aware, during the time, that I was earning Mr. Thiel's respect. As he was, I must own, earning mine. We were not companionable, and I certainly did not feel I knew him well, but as long as the conversation stayed away from personal subjects he was willing to continue it. I myself had some interest in learning how his mind worked, and moreover, it seemed to me that if I listened carefully I might glimpse something of what he kept so carefully hidden. Sundays, when I returned from the Callenders', Mr. Thiel and I would sit in the kitchen over a dinner he had prepared and talk about education, art, the nature of man. These conversations did not bubble or flow, they were halting, serious affairs. Most often, they began with a question I would ask. "Why do people give alms to beggars?" or "Did any of the African missionaries speak the language of the people among whom they went?" Mr. Thiel's concern was not for the specific question, although he answered it thoughtfully as a rule, but for the general principle behind it. Often we had a fundamental disagreement and would find ourselves arguing the point from opposite sides. He assumed not only superior knowledge, but also superior understanding, which galled me. Often, I would be lying in my own bed before the proper response came to me; sometimes I even came to agree with him. I never told him this, of course; it wouldn't have been wise, I knew instinctively, to let him feel he was winning me over. I needed to be as wary with him as he was with me.

Between those two, Sundays went quickly by, in anticipation, memory and enjoyment. I wrote to Aunt Constance about those days more than any others.

Mr. Thiel and I did have dinner with the McWilliams family, which I recall in colors of warm kerosene lamps and tones of ordinary voices, talking, laughing, quarreling. In that sprawling village house, the children dominated a room, although they obeyed their elders quickly enough. Mac had four younger sisters, each of whom claimed part of my attention. The adults sat quietly, talking in lazy tones of unimportant matters. In that house, I was one among many children, which I found restful. I ran about among the rooms, took part in silly games and enjoyed myself. Mac sometimes played with us, and sometimes sat beside his father, silently listening.

Those weeks were a happy time for me. As Aunt Constance had predicted, I was doing well. I could feel my mind and spirits expanding, not physically, but in experience. I realized that I had led a sheltered life until then, and—while I did not resent the narrowness of my Cambridge life—I was glad to learn more, to broaden my knowledge of the world. And to expand it in so many different ways at the same time.

During that time, too, I went through more and more of the boxes, with increased efficiency and curiosity. In the second week of August, I began on the final box. There had been no repetition of the nightmare. I suspect that was because I felt I was doing something about the problem. My mind was at ease because I was dealing with it. Thus, the terror of it was put into a place where I could manage it, and it did not need to creep out in dreams. I had determined to work steadily, confident of my ability to recognize whatever it was Mr. Thiel intended me to find, or not to find, when I saw it.

As if to reward my careful, patient work (and I felt I deserved a reward because I *had* been so impatient to get to the final box), I found a note from Irene to her father. There was no date on it, but it must have been written after Mrs. Bywall's theft:

> *Dear Father,* [she wrote]
>   *I am writing this late at night. I know you will read and think about it carefully, and you know that I will abide by your decision. I ask you, this last time, to reconsider the changes in your will. You must disapprove of Enoch's determination to prosecute; I understand that. However, whatever you will think of him, he is your son and entitled to benefit from our wealth. Whatever he is, you and I are responsible for him, and responsible to him. I don't think we can avoid the truth of that. For myself, you know how little I need. Enoch needs more, whether for good or ill I will not judge. My only concern is for our baby, you know that, and you know what steps I have taken for the child's care and safety. I beg you to think once more what good will come from your proposed will? And think further, what evil?*

I studied this note. Its firm handwriting sloped forward without curlicues and fanciness. Mr. Callender had said something about a will. Mr. Thiel had said that he, Mr. Callender that is, received an allowance. I wondered what the will had actually said, what provisions it made. I decided to ask Aunt Constance about it, not immediately, of course, but at a time when she might be disposed to answer. But there might be ways to find out what the will said. Somebody had to know that.

Poor Irene, poor Mrs. Thiel, so sure that she had taken good care of her child. I was glad she did not know what had happened. But I wondered why she had been worried about her child's safety.

Chapter Eleven

*I*t was after one of those pleasant Sundays, toward the middle of August, that I awoke in the dead still of night. For a moment, or even less time, I lay bewildered. A dream? A noise? What had wakened me?

I was seized by pain, as if a fire scorched my stomach. The sharp pain caused me to turn over in bed and gasp. Flaming waves of pain passed across my stomach, one following the other, and then, finally, they abated. For a time I lay back in my bed, exhausted, panting.

I thought at first, while I could still think clearly, that I would stay in bed and let whatever the illness was run its course. I did not want to waken Mr. Thiel. I was embarrassed. I thought that if it became necessary I would find Mrs. Bywall. A woman is always less of a stranger than a man. I wished I could have been in Cambridge, with Aunt Constance next door.

Two more attacks of this pain left me weak and almost weeping. Pain, I discovered, is terrible. It can change your ideas. Now I wanted only someone, anyone, just any relief. All of my attention was devoured by the pain. I no longer cared for being embarrassed, or for anything else. And the attacks seemed to be getting worse, not better.

I forced myself out of bed and into the hallway. There I called out, softly at first, then loudly. That is the last thing I remember clearly. After that there was only the pain itself and voices around me. Mr. Thiel's face, Mrs. Bywall's face and her arms holding me down in my bed while her voice said something about "just a little while" as she bathed my forehead with a damp cloth.

Dr. McWilliams's round head appeared above my bed, but he was not smiling. He forced me to swallow something. I vomited. Then I fainted or slept or did both in that order—I cannot remember.

It was late morning when I awoke for the second time. Mrs. Bywall sat by my bed. The room was filled with sunlight. She was knitting something shapeless. Her face looked tired, but she actually smiled at me. "Awake, are you? How do you feel?"

"Tired . . . and weak, but better."

"Let me call the doctor," she said, putting down her knitting.

I found it beyond my strength to protest, although I could think quite clearly that this was too much trouble. Mrs. Bywall read my mind. "He's just downstairs, talking with Mr. Thiel. He's been waiting for you to wake up. He said you would soon. He thought you might be hungry. I'll bring you a cup of tea and some dry toast." She leaned over me and straightened the bedclothes. "You gave us a proper fright," she said, "and your hair needs brushing." While she did that, I noticed that I was wearing a fresh nightgown. My mouth felt stiff and swollen. My stomach, when I pressed gently on it, was sore, as if bruised. Mrs. Bywall brushed my hair briskly, braided it, then left the room.

Dr. McWilliams smiled quite cheerfully at me. "Better now? I thought so. Let me just look at you while Mrs. Bywall gets you something to eat."

Once I had swallowed a little tea and toast, I felt better, stronger, and more able to talk. Dr. McWilliams sat and watched me eat, nodding in satisfaction.

"What did I have?" I finally asked.

"I'm not quite sure," he said. "I need your help to find out. Tell me what happened."

I told him about waking up and the fiery waves of pain. It is hard to remember pain and to describe it accurately, once you are feeling well again. Dr. McWilliams listened carefully and asked no questions.

"Something you ate seems to have disagreed with you," he said.

The understatement made me smile.

"Our task is to find out what it was. Did you have anything yesterday you have never eaten before?"

I thought back. "No," I said.

"Any berries you found? Nuts? Any wild fruit?"

"No," I said.

"Well then, can you remember what you had for meals yesterday?" He took out a little notebook and apologized, "I'll never remember If I don't write it down."

"For breakfast, pancakes with butter and syrup, milk, and a bowl of applesauce," I began.

"Did you put any sugar on your applesauce?" he interrupted.

"No. For lunch a boiled chicken, carrots, biscuits and gravy. A bread pudding. Water. For supper fish, boiled potatoes, chard, tomatoes and some leftover cherry pie. Milk, I think. I had a cup of sweet tea afterwards."

"Was there anything you ate that nobody else ate?" he asked.

"I don't think so. Oh, the tea."

"What does sweet tea mean? Sugar and milk?"

"Yes."

"Did anybody else have sugar?"

"I don't think so. It's in the sugar bowl on the table. The kitchen table."

"Milk?"

"That's in the pitcher in the springhouse. Mr. Thiel had some too, with his dinner. He always does."

"Probably not bad milk then," Dr. McWilliams said. "Mr. Thiel may have been a frightened man last night, but he wasn't a sick one. Nobody who was sick could have covered as much ground as he did, as quickly as he did."

He sat and studied his notes. I thought my own thoughts.

"The question is what you ate that nobody else would have tasted," he said. "The tea is one. The syrup at breakfast?"

"No," I said, "we all had some of that. Anything from a glass, though, is that what you mean?" He nodded. "The baked pudding was in individual cups. But I didn't eat much of it. It was lumpy, terrible."

"Was it baked in the cups? Or just served in them."

"Baked in them, I think."

"What makes you think that?"

"When we washed up, there was no pudding bowl to put away."

"Anything else?"

"My tea."

"Do you usually have a cup of tea in the evenings?"

"Often, not always. I make it myself."

He closed his notebook and looked at me for a long time. I looked steadily back at him. "Whatever it was," he said, "you've come through it all right. So that's good. What I did was give you huge dose of Ipecacuana—you know what that is?"

"A purge?"

"Yes. It emptied your stomach."

"I remember," I said.

"It's an extreme step but in your case it was necessary."

"It wasn't a disease, was it," I said.

"No. No, I'm afraid I don't think it was. As to what happened, exactly, I can't be sure. Something didn't agree with you, something you ate, that much we can be sure of. The question is, just what was it? And how did it get into your stomach?"

I had an idea, but was afraid to mention it. Sometimes, it is as if things will not be real unless you speak of them.

"There are two possibilities," Dr. McWilliams said. He came and sat beside me on the bed. He took my hands in his. "One possibility is that there was some natural poison in something you ate, some food turned bad, yet not bad enough to taste. So you wouldn't notice it as you ate. The other possibility is—some unnatural poison."

He had spoken my fear aloud.

"Who would want to do that to me?" I asked.

"I don't know," he shook his head. "It doesn't make sense to me. You're only a child, and a stranger here. Is there anything about you I don't know? Is there any reason you might be in danger?"

"No," I said. I had only vague surmises. I couldn't tell him of these.

"Then I think we can assume that you had a bit of unusually bad luck, don't you?" I didn't answer. "I want you to stay in bed today and eat lightly but as often as you want. Tomorrow you should keep quietly inside. Shall I send Mac up to you in the afternoon tomorrow? Will a lesson with him distract you?"

"I'd like that," I said.

Dr. McWilliams stood up. "I pronounce you well," he said solemnly, "but remember that you are convalescent for a couple of days. You will behave yourself, won't you?"

"Of course," I said.

"I thought so. You seem a sensible child. Mac says you've got a good head on your shoulders." I flushed with pleasure.

After he had left, Mrs. Bywall returned. She saw that I had not finished the breakfast tray and sat down with her knitting. She pulled out the needles and began to unravel and wind the yarn.

"What are you doing?" I asked. "Why are you doing that?"

"Oh. I only knit when I'm worried. I can't do it properly, you know, knitting. So I have a ball of wool I save for occasions."

"And I haven't even thanked you properly," I said.

"That's not necessary. I'm used to sickbeds. They're no trouble," she answered. "For a bit there you had us really worried. When he heard you, we both came running. Dr. McWilliams said it's lucky you came out for help." She studied my face for a long time. "You'll be hungry, I expect, in a little while. How does some good broth sound?"

It sounded delicious and I told her so. "What happened last night?" I asked. "I can't remember much."

"Well—Mr. Thiel woke up and I woke up. He was lifting you when I got there, to take you to your room. I stayed with you. He rode off for the doctor and they rode back like the devil was after them. Dr. McWilliams thought appendicitis at first, but it didn't take him long to change his mind. He gave you some medicine—"

"I remember that," I said. I didn't see any need to cover that again.

"Well, then you got easier, it seemed. You quieted.

132

Finally you slept. The men went down to the library and I sat here with you. You slept well."

"Thank you," I said. When you are truly, deeply grateful, those words cannot say enough. Perhaps deep gratitude, like deep joy, is impossible to express.

"Mr. Thiel asked if he could visit for a minute. He's right outside."

"Of course," I said.

Mr. Thiel, like Mrs. Bywall, looked tired. I guessed that Dr. McWilliams was more accustomed to staying up all night. I thanked him, too, for his care. He dismissed it with a rough gesture of his hands.

"I've some books here you might want to read. You're not to go downstairs today," he said.

"So Dr. McWilliams told me."

"I'll be out for a bit this afternoon, but Mrs. Bywall will sit with you. Do you know how to play cribbage? Then we might have a game later. I've no idea how to entertain an invalid." He seemed cross about that.

"I'm not an invalid," I protested.

"No, I guess that's so, and a good thing. Well then—" and he left, having come no further into the room than the door.

I spent a lot of time that day lying in bed with an unread book open before me, thinking carefully. My first idea was to return to Aunt Constance, to go home. But by daylight the room was familiar and safe. It was illogical to think that somebody would try to kill me. There was no reason for it. However, that Dr. McWilliams had even considered the idea was enough to terrify me. It was like living within the dream world of a nightmare—only you couldn't wake up.

Think carefully, I reminded myself. As Dr. McWilliams had said, I was a stranger here. There must have been something turned bad in something I ate. Perhaps all of the Callenders had also been ill during the night. Was that possible? Unreasonably, I though it was not; somehow I was convinced of the singularity of my illness. Mr. Thiel had not been ill. Mrs. Bywall had not. It was only me.

Why? What made me different from everybody else? I assumed that someone had tried to poison me and tried to think of any possible motive for it. The only thing I did that was different from everybody else was my work. Those papers again. Was there something in the papers? Could somebody know how far I had gotten? Mac knew. Anybody who looked in the library would know, because the boxes I had completed were neatly rearranged and labeled. That is, anybody who had access to the library, anybody in this house. Then, was there something in the final box somebody wanted to conceal? Of course that argument was built on the assumption that I had been deliberately poisoned, which was not a reasonable assumption.

I wanted to find the will, Mr. Callender's will. When Mrs. Bywall brought me a tray of tea and white rolls during the afternoon ("I thought perhaps jam wouldn't be too heavy for your stomach," she said, settling down in her chair again) I asked her:

"Do you know what was in Mr. Callender's will?"

"Josiah Callender? No, I don't know." She hesitated before adding, "I don't know that anybody does, except Mr. Enoch and I guess Mr. Thiel. I wasn't here then, remember. It was years later when I returned, and everything was as it is now. What are you thinking of?" Her eyes studied me.

"Nothing," I said.

"No, I remember. When I first got back I was surprised that Mr. Callender was still here. I knew his father and sister had died, and I thought he would have moved away, with nothing to hold him here. He never liked Marlborough. And poor Mrs. Callender would do anything he wanted. I thought he'd be long gone. Could that have anything to do with a will?"

"I don't know," I said.

"Mr. Thiel would know," she said, "but I wouldn't dare ask him. He'd not like it."

"I know," I said.

It was while I played cribbage with Mr. Thiel that I thought of something I had forgotten. The reason cribbage is a relaxing game, suitable for the bedridden, is that it depends largely on luck. Therefore, it doesn't take much attention. While we played, my mind was busy working. It was as I was counting out one hand, saying "fifteen two, four, six and the pair makes ten" that I remembered the locked drawer in the desk. I realized, at the same time, that I knew nothing about breaking into locked drawers but that Mac might, and he would be visiting tomorrow afternoon.

Mr. Thiel, sitting on a chair by the bed, didn't notice my distraction. Perhaps he too was distracted. At the end of the hand, he didn't shuffle the cards. Instead, he looked at me and said, "Dr. McWilliams spoke to you? About the possibility of poison?"

"Yes." I was startled to hear him mention it. Having it stated in that way made the fears return. "It seems impossible," I said, not as confidently as I could have wished. I tried not to let him see my fear.

"Yes, it does," he said. His expression was hard and serious, as if he were measuring me. "Some impossible things do happen."

"I know," I said, calmly, coldly. It wouldn't do to let him see my suspicions.

"I wondered if you wanted to return to Cambridge," he said.

"I considered that," I answered. "I wish Aunt Constance were here. She'd know what to do."

"I have written to her," Mr. Thiel said. "I think I know what she will say. If I were sure she was right. . . . But how do you feel about it? Frightened?"

"Yes," I said. I could say that much; he would be more suspicious were I to deny it.

"It could have been bad food," he said.

"That is the only sensible, logical thing," I agreed.

"If not—it was either here or there," he said.

I knew what he meant: either someone in this house or in the other house had tired to poison me. I knew, further, that he was one of those whom I must suspect, but I could not tell if he knew I knew it.

"There was nothing odd about your visit yesterday?" he asked.

"No, nothing at all. We ate, talked, and Mr. Callender walked me back."

"To the falls?"

Perhaps I should have lied to him at that point and told him we crossed at the ford, but I didn't. I stared helplessly into his dark eyes. I couldn't tell the truth. I couldn't lie.

"I've always assumed you crossed on that little bridge my wife told me of," Mr. Thiel said.

"I didn't know anyone knew," I said. "He told me it was a secret."

"As far as he knows, it is," Mr. Thiel said. "Irene told me. Then, yesterday, you came straight back here. Was everything normal here?"

"Wasn't it?" I asked. I was uncomfortable.

"I'm asking for your impression of things," he said.

"I thought so."

"I don't like it," Mr. Thiel said. "I wish you had eaten some green apples or wild berries."

"So do I," I said. Suddenly I was exhausted, my weakened will dizzied by the conversation with my employer, like a sparring match, or a duel of wills between wary opponents.

"Mrs. Bywall has asked to sleep in here with you tonight. Shall I let her? Or are you too old for that? I know so little about children. We could easily put a cot in here for her."

I couldn't answer, except to nod my head. I didn't know whether I should accept the offer or not. I didn't know where safety lay, or if there was any real danger. I only knew I had dreaded being alone during the night.

The next afternoon Mac and I, with the help of a pocket knife, opened the drawer.

"What are you looking for?" he asked, as we heard the lock slip into place, releasing the drawer. "Why don't you just ask for the key?"

"I'll tell you after we see what's there," I said.

He pulled the drawer out and we both leaned over it. It was empty.

Mac put his hand into it, felt back to every corner, and then closed the drawer. He couldn't relock it. I could only hope that nobody would notice. "Well?" he asked me.

I was too surprised to speak. I don't know exactly what I had expected to find in there. A copy of the will, or some correspondence about it. Something to clear up the darkness and mystery.

"You said you'd explain," Mac reminded me.

I looked at his round face and earnest eyes and decided to trust him. I had to trust somebody. I had to talk to somebody. I was becoming muddleheaded with fear and puzzlement. He, at least, could have been in no way involved in those events of ten years ago. Although, I reminded myself, he was Mr. Thiel's friend and he disliked Mr. Callender; he wasn't impartial.

"You'll keep it secret," I cautioned.

His eyes lit up. "I promise," he said. "Cross my heart."

"I was looking for the will, Mr. Callender's will."

"Josiah Callender?"

"Yes. I found a note from his daughter to him about

137

changes in it she didn't want him to make—changes against Mr. Callender. Mr. Enoch Callender," I added.

"When was this note written?"

"It wasn't dated. But it was in this last box."

"So, it was close to when she died," Mac said.

I nodded.

"Do you think that that might be the reason she died—she was murdered?"

"Yes. No. I don't know. But don't you see, if we knew what the will said, then we would know who inherited the fortune. And we would know if anyone had a motive."

"Not necessarily," Mac pointed out. "It would depend on the person knowing what the will said. And when the will was signed."

"If it was actually drawn up," I added. "Josiah Callender may have decided to do as his daughter asked and not cut out Mr. Callender."

"That wouldn't solve the real mystery anyway," Mac said.

"What is that?"

"How she was killed."

"I think I know," I said.

For a minute, I enjoyed his surprise.

"There's a bridge, a sort of bridge, over the falls. Mr. Callender showed it to me. It's a board he hides in the trees on his side. I cross over it when I return from his side of the stream. You place it over the falls, he stands on it to steady it, and you can walk across."

"That means Mr. Callender is the one." Mac stated it calmly, but his excitement showed in his eyes.

"Mr. Thiel knew about it too," I said. "He told me yesterday."

"Either one of them." Mac was equally calm about this. "Then, if Mr. Thiel inherited the money from his wife, he would have a motive. If Mr. Callender would lose the money by her death, he wouldn't kill her, would he? But if there was a new will, and it hadn't been signed yet, Mr. Callender *would* have a motive. I see what you mean, we need to see the will."

"There's something else too," I said.

"What's that?"

"In her note, Irene said that the child would be safe, that she had seen to that. As if the child—" I hesitated. "And then, the child disappeared." The whole thing was such a huge tangle of possibilities that I had a strange desire to giggle. Mac's face was serious though. "Why should someone try to poison you?" he asked.

"We don't know that anyone did," I said. "Does your father think someone did? For sure? That's not what he told me."

"He's not absolutely sure either," Mac said.

All of my vague fears returned. I did not want to worry about that illness—I wanted to throw myself into the search for the will and solving the Callender mystery.

"The only thing I can think of to do is look for the will, or some information in the papers," I said weakly. "If somebody knows there's something there, something they want kept secret, something they're afraid I'll find . . . if I find it then there wouldn't be any reason to try to stop me anymore. Would there?"

"Then let's get to it," Mac said. He looked at the stacks of paper on the long table and sighed. "It can't be worse than Caesar after all."

Chapter Twelve

S_o much happened in that final week, I have trouble keeping track of the days. It was Sunday evening that I was—ill. The Monday I spent in bed. Tuesday Mac came, and I confided in him and he became an ally. So much an ally that on Wednesday morning he arrived to help me go through the final box of papers. All of those nights Mrs. Bywall slept with me, and whenever I awoke, her low snoring lulled me to sleep again. You may think it strange that a woman with her past could still be a comfort. I trusted her.

I could not then have said why I trusted her and found her sleeping form a guardian against the nightmares, against the black shape that appeared and reappeared in my dreams. The shape came closer each time, until I could almost see his face within the dark folds of cloth; each night he forced me to return with him to the glade, pulled me up the edge of the falls. Then he stood across the board from me and held out his hand. At those times, there was nobody waiting in the deep pool and the dark wind whipped my dress around my ankles. I knew then whose body lay at the base of the falls, but the phantom pulled me out onto the board, even so. The water rushed below my bare feet. Once, a woman's form rose up from below and her arms stretched out as if to embrace me. I awoke, then, shaking, my hand tight over my mouth. Mrs. Bywall's snores, at those times, sounded in my ears like music—the monotonous, rasping noise in the darkness enabled me to close my eyes.

Things were happening too fast for careful thought. My nights were without rest. During my waking hours I felt perpetually off-balance. At any moment I might fall over, tumbling helplessly into danger. I knew that. What I might find at the end of that fall frightened me too much to think about it.

That Wednesday morning I had just begun to work in the library when Mrs. Bywall showed Mac in. I gave him a pile of papers and we both set to work. Mac was restless. Although he remained in his chair, he squirmed and fidgeted. He ruffled through the pile to see how many he had left to do. Once he looked up at me, after only half an hour it was, and remarked, "I was wrong, it *is* worse than Caesar." But he kept at it.

After the disappointment of the drawer, I didn't really expect to find anything, and I was not disappointed in that expectation. I kept on just to be doing something. There were more lists, an itinerary of the objects in the house (including various baby items like porringers and spoons, which meant that we had progressed to 1882 or 1883). I asked Mac when a baby would need those things, and he explained to me that they were probably presented at birth. He began to make a long explanation of when they were first used by a child and to deduce from that the most exact dating, but I gazed at him sternly. He sighed and returned to the business of reading.

Among the order lists for a store in Boston and letters from stockbrokers in that city, I did find another note in Irene Callender Thiel's slanted handwriting. It was a personal note, almost a love letter, and it seemed to me to match the earnest child's face I had seen in the portrait at Mr. Callender's house.

> *Dan,* [it began]
> *I hope all goes well with Mr. Rogers. You will remember to thank Constance for me, especially for me? It may be that he will not like your pictures, or will not find them salable. But it is a great opportunity for you. You do not have to thank Constance for yourself, if you don't care to. She will understand. (You two do seem to have an excellent understanding.) Sometimes I wonder if she would not be a better wife for you, both of you knowing so surely what is right. I am a quieter creature, and so indecisive! My heart rules my head. Then I sit beside our child, who reaches out to me with such small hands . . . and I see in my memory your own hands, with the little fingers wrapped around yours . . . and I am confident, contented. Remember, the softest wool you can find (take Constance with you, you are too impatient to choose carefully enough) and the most beautiful toy, if you insist on it. I know you, you will insist; but you must promise me to heed Constance's advice, which will be good.*

The note was signed only "with love." It was also, clearly, written with love. I was moved by it. The voice of the woman ten years dead was real in it. I felt a sense of grief, as if I had lost her myself.

Mac distracted me by shoving a piece of paper before my eyes. "I can't make any sense out of this, can you?" he asked.

It was a rough-edged, irregular sheet, apparently scratch

paper, filled with capital letters and arrows, separated into four sections.

"It's a geometry problem or something," Mac said. "How can you spend a whole summer doing this kind of work?"

I was studying the paper. "I think it's the will," I said. I was quite calm. Mac was not.

"You think so? You really think so? You mean we did it? Jean, what's the matter with you—you don't even look pleased. It's the *will*." He seized the paper and took it to the window. His face fell. "It can't be," he said. "Wills are long and complicated."

"It's an outline," I explained patiently. "Look—LWT would be Last Will and Testament. The section headed *P*. would be private or perpetual or permanent or personal bequests. Something like that, because he must have had people or institutions he wanted to leave money to, servants or charities. This section leaves everything to Irene—she'd be Irene Thiel wouldn't she? That's IT, isn't it? and something for J, that's Joseph Callender; V, Victoria; B, Benjamin; and J."

"Two for Joseph?"

"Probably not."

"Couldn't it have been the initial of the child? Irene Thiel's child?" Mac asked. "Lots of names begin with J, James, John, Janet, Jessica, you can spell Jeff with a J. What do you think EC means? with PC crossed out?" Mac went on.

"PC has been added above in that section, see? maybe an allowance? Mr. Thiel said Mr. Callender had one."

I was still working my way through the initials, when Mac said, "I understand it." He had been standing beside me while I followed the arrows through, decoding names, trying to make all the parts of each individual section clear.

"Listen," Mac said. "He left it to his daughter. If she died before him (which wasn't likely, was it?), then the money would be split between the two families, with Mr. Thiel as trustee for all of it. See? So if his daughter was dead, then Mr. Callender got half in trust, so just the income, and this JT got the other half. If Mr. Callender died, his children got his half. So he left it to her first, then to the grandchildren. And if everybody died, he was going to give it to the institutions he had circled. I wonder how much there was. Don't you?"

Mac had grasped the major plan before I had begun to know it was there.

"This," he pointed to the bracketed section, "must be the terms of Irene Thiel's will, which leaves everything to her child or—if the child is dead—to her brother. With no trustee."

I added a detail: "So that Mr. Callender is never a trustee and Mr. Thiel never inherits."

He nodded.

"If that's what it is," I said, "then what happened? Mr. Callender, Josiah Callender, died. Irene inherited." My finger traced this progress on the paper. "When she died, her child inherited."

"With Mr. Thiel as trustee," Mac added.

"And when the child disappeared?" I asked.

"If he's alive," Mac thought aloud, "then he inherits it all. If he is dead, Mr. Callender does."

"And if nobody knows whether he's alive or dead, then everything has to stay the same, doesn't it?" I concluded. "Mr. Thiel has the money now, in a way. Because he is the trustee. So he's inherited, or as good as."

"Yes," Mac said. "But after a person has been missing for seven years you can have him declared legally dead. Why wouldn't Mr. Thiel do that?"

We were silent again. Mac started the next train of thought. "If Irene Thiel was murdered—it would be because the murderer wanted that second version of the will, where the fortune was split equally. If she was murdered, it would be because she was supposed to die before her father, and the money would be split between the two families, with Mr. Thiel in control of it."

"We haven't solved anything, have we?" I realized. "We only have two real choices for people with motives; and they both profit from the second version of the will."

Mac looked at me: "I don't know how you can be so cool-headed about this."

I wasn't cool-headed, if he had known. My mind was in a turmoil. I was just holding onto what facts we had, as a drowning man must hold onto a life preserver.

"Then," I continued, "the real question isn't about the death of Irene Thiel, it's about the child. First, what happened to him? Second, why was no investigation made? Third, why wasn't he declared legally dead?"

Mrs. Bywall opened the door then, to announce lunch. "Mr. Thiel thought you would be staying," she told Mac.

"Yes, thank you," Mac said, with a glance at me out of the side of his eyes. He seemed embarrassed.

"What have the two of you been doing here? You look like the cat that ate the canary, the both of you. Mr. Thiel is already at table," she warned us.

We returned the paper to its place in the pile. It had lain there so long unnoticed, I assumed it would be safe.

Something, I thought to myself, should be safe. I did not feel safe. I was confused and disturbed. The nightmare seemed to be seeping over into the daylight hours: just beyond the edges of my vision, shadowy shapes moved, Irene Thiel, this child, the nurse into whose care Mr. Thiel had placed the child, Mr. Thiel himself as his wife wrote to him, Mr. Callender trying to hold his sister's affections, and old Josiah Callender himself, trying to do the right thing with his fortune, who would perhaps have known his family best, who apparently trusted neither his son nor his son-in-law.

That lunch was not a comfortable meal for me. Mac ate away as if nothing were wrong. Mr. Thiel was even more quiet than usual. I could not look at him, but could not look away. I wanted him to speak, to say anything, to convince him of the normality of things, but everytime he spoke I was thrown into a panic and could think of no reply. I ate little, and quickly.

"Didn't your aunt teach you the manners to clean your plate?" Mr. Thiel said.

I glared at him. It was none of his business. "Won't your mother worry if you aren't home for lunch?" I asked Mac, ignoring Mr. Thiel.

"Why should she? She knows where I am," Mac answered.

"How could she know you'd stay to lunch?" I insisted.

"Well, she told me I could stay as long as I liked. She said she didn't mind, for this while."

"So you're here to keep an eye on me," I said. He looked uncomfortable and his eyes turned to Mr. Thiel. For some reason, that made me angry. It was not just a foot-stamping anger, it was a hot, burning wrath. I looked at the two of them. Mr. Thiel was about to say something, I could tell. I didn't wait to hear what it was.

"I don't need anybody to look after me," I said coldly, to both of them. "Nobody looked after me before, did they? This sudden concern for my well-being—"

I couldn't think of anything scathing enough, so I didn't finish my sentence. Quite calmly, I folded my napkin and rose from the table. Quite calmly, I walked out of the dining room and then out of the house. Then I began to run wildly, before my tears could be noticed by anyone following me. I ran up into the woods toward the falls.

Chapter Thirteen

B_y the time I had crossed at the ford, then walked down to Mr. Callender's house, I had ceased sobbing. I imagine I looked pretty disheveled, however: I'd left shoes and stockings by the stream and run through the forested countryside, not bothering to avoid bushes. Mr. Callender took one look at me and knelt down beside me. "My dear," he said. His eyes looked gently into mine. "What has happened?"

I shook my head, I could not have begun to explain to him why I was there. I did not understand it myself. I had only feelings: I felt alone, afraid; I felt angry at everyone, and as if things were happening that I did not understand; I felt helpless.

Mr. Callender stared into my face. "Has he been cruel to you? Don't try to pretend, I know how miserable my sister's life was with him. Whatever it is, Jean, it will be set right."

That was what pulled me out of it, because I knew—not only felt, but knew, as a fact—that everything was not all right and never could be. He must have seen something in my face.

"Better?" he asked.

I had found him leaving his house, outside, alone. He was kneeling so that his face was even with mine. His voice was soothing, comforting; but his eyes bored into mine as if to read my mind. "What did happen?" He gave me his handkerchief. I blew my nose several times.

"Nothing," I said, remembering that I did not know who could be trusted. I thought of something to satisfy him, "I was ill, some kind of food poisoning. I wasn't sure you all were well."

That did surprise him. I am sure of it, or, at least, I was sure of it then. "As you see," he said, "I am in perfect health. So are the rest of us, I promise you. When was this?"

"Sunday."

"Is everyone well at the big house? Did you have the doctor?"

Yes, I nodded. "But I'm sorry, you were going downtown. I've interrupted."

"That isn't important. That will wait for another day. Shall we walk? Where we won't be disturbed? You seem to me to be a young lady in need of a friend." He stood up and dusted the dirt from his knees. He looked back at his house, but there was nobody to be seen, and we went back, slowly, by the path upriver.

"You really *don't* want to talk to me?" he asked gently. "You can tell me anything, anything. I want to be your friend. But you don't want to talk, and I can understand that. What you want—let me guess—is simply the comfort of a friend. Just to walk along as we are now, talking of other things, so that you can forget, however temporarily, whatever troubles you."

He seemed to know so much about me, I could only be grateful.

"You're still a child, after all." He smiled down at me. His hair glowed golden in the sunlight, and his eyes shone a dark, kindly blue. "You're so composed, one tends to forget that. Under your cool exterior you have plenty of feelings, haven't you?"

I agreed, embarrassed.

"I'm so glad you feel you can come to me for comfort," he said. "I think I am beginning to understand you. My sister Irene, she too had deep feelings, which she disguised. I always knew that. Other people never seemed to notice what she was really like. Your Mr. Thiel, he never even suspected it. Poor Irene."

"What was she like, your sister?" I asked him. I felt now that of all the Callenders, she was the one I liked most, even more (strange as it may seem) than Mr. Enoch Callender.

"She was tall and dark, not pretty at all. But she was the most loyal person you'd ever hope to meet, and kindness itself. She never mixed well in company, always standing back—she was so awkward, it made her shy—and then when a man came courting she was too intelligent not to know he was courting her money. Sometimes she would ask me what I thought of this one or that one. I wouldn't try to lie, I loved her too much to lie to her. And I said that and told her that I for one wouldn't change a single thing about her, not for all the engagement rings set out in Mr. Tiffany's counters. Many's the time she helped me out of one scrape or another, Irene. She could talk to me, make me see reason when nobody else could. I knew I could trust her, you see, that's the kind of person she was. If she told me not to do something, I always thought twice about it." He smiled at the memory. "I didn't always do what she asked, but even then she never held that against me, never carried a grudge. She didn't want me to marry my wife."

"Why not?" I asked.

"She thought I was too young, and she might have been right. Then she said Priscilla wasn't strong enough, that Priscilla loved me too much—and she was correct, of course. I quickly learned what Irene had meant. But my sister never gloated. She just helped whenever she could, with money or little attentions. She listened to Priscilla's little tales of woe. Whereas my father—" His voice became bitter. Until then, as he spoke of his sister, his voice had sounded happy.

"Your father?" I asked him.

"My dear father said that Priscilla wasn't rich enough to keep me. I pointed out to him that he could do something about that, but he wouldn't. I was young and in love; I didn't obey him. Then, afterwards, he said we'd made our bed and now we had to lie on it. Irene used to come over and help Priscilla with the household accounts, advise her how to handle the cook and maids, even the children. Priscilla has never been able to manage. Irene took care of the children, she was wonderful with them. Of course, all that changed when she married."

"Why did it change? You lived here, nearby, didn't you?"

Mr. Callender looked down at me with a twinkle in his blue eyes. "Don't tell me you haven't noticed. I don't try to disguise it, you don't have to pretend with me. There is no love lost between your employer and myself. Come now, Jean, you can speak the truth with me."

"Oh that," I said. "Yes, I knew that."

"My sister changed," Mr. Callender said. "My poor, gentle sister, married to a man who had been a Hider, who cared for nothing but his paintings. In her unhappiness, she grew distant. The man has never thought of anyone but himself, you must have remarked that in him—" He did not wait for me to answer. "And that little child—perhaps it is just as well—imagine being left alone with him in that house. Imagine the long hours of each long day, or having to turn to him in need. I could have done little good for the child: he won't have me in the house. Not that I want to go. But even so, when I think—I even tried to trace her, which is more than the father did."

"You tried?"

"Under the terms of my father's will, my wife received an inheritance. I hired detectives. It wasn't very much money, it didn't last long. They had simply disappeared, the child and that unknown nurse, both of them. I insisted that the detectives keep on looking—I was quite frantic—following up any clue, until the money ran out. He wouldn't give me any more."

"You hate Mr. Thiel," I said. I had not understood that before.

"What do you expect, when he ruined my life for me. You may not know that I have an allowance, under my rich father's generous will"—the bitterness was in his voice again—"which Mr. Thiel doles out to me in bits and pieces. Twice a week I present myself to a teller at the bank, with my hand out. We are trapped here. I am trapped. And there is all that money. . . ."

His eyes glittered icy blue when he spoke of the money. We had arrived at the ford and sat down side by side on a wide boulder. He continued talking, almost as if he were talking to someone who knew him better than I did, to someone who had known him all his life and was familiar with the intricacies of his character.

"After all, there's more than one way to live. For people with imagination and bold spirits, life offers so much. Irene understood that, and she understood me. And she died." He hit at his knees with a fist. "And here I am.

"The son should inherit. I would have let them live with us, I would have taken care of her, of them. Even him, since she would have wanted that. And I had plans, good ones; they couldn't have failed. I wanted to buy back the munitions factory. There are always places in the world where guns and powder are needed, because men will always behave, alas, like murderers and warmongers. You just have to see that, and your fortune is made. Granted, some of my associates were of the wrong sort—I knew that. But I never tried to introduce them into my home. I was always discreet. These men had ideas, ideas that only needed a capital investment. It would never have touched my family, not the precious Callenders. I would have seen to that."

He stopped talking abruptly, as if he had noticed that it was I who sat listening. "Whatever do you make of all that, Miss Jean Wainwright? What would you do with a brother like me?" He smiled, but his eyes stayed icy.

It was a test. I could feel that. He seemed to care intensely for what I would answer. The broad stream ran in front of us, and overhead the branches of the trees whispered. I thought how solitary Mr. Callender's life must be, for him to be at all concerned about my opinion. He was a man removed from his natural habitat, trying to live in an uncongenial environment. I thought carefully as he waited for my response—but I was not thinking about what I would say. I thought instead of how Aunt Constance had spoken of the beauty of these mountains, and how Mr. Thiel had painted all the strength of the landscape without losing its loveliness. I thought about Mr. Callender, beside me, sitting within a ring of hills whose rise and fall was both symmetrical and irregular, sitting upon a boulder so large and hard it looked as if it had thrust its own way up out of the very earth. Mr. Callender wore a fresh linen suit, his boots were polished to a high gleam, his golden head bent down to study the toes.

There were facts he had told me that did not match facts I had learned from the Callender papers. *Was* his sister unhappy? Was Mr. Thiel such a man as he had claimed? Was Mr. Callender's allowance ungenerous? Was his face, as I had seen its change of expression when he spoke of the fortune, was that the face of greed? At last I answered him. "I don't know."

That was as much of a lie as I could manage. Of course, I did know. I would do just as Irene Thiel had done: I would be troubled and uneasy, I would be as generous as I thought sensible, but I would be unable to trust him. I would have to love him, but I would not trust him. It was a terrible thought.

But Mr. Callender insisted that I answer fully. "You're not being truthful with me."

I looked at him and felt tears fill my eyes. He was, possibly, a wonderful man, a man with many gifts, with grace and wit, an informed mind, a man who might make joyful any place where he lived. What did he lack that made me know he was not to be trusted?

"I would take care of such a brother," I said. "I would do everything I could to help him be the best sort of man he could be."

He laughed then. "Do you know? Good people are all alike, their minds cast from a single mold."

"I don't understand," I said.

"You don't need to, and I don't think you ever can," he told me.

"I've made you angry," I said. "I don't want to make you angry."

"How could you make me angry by telling me the truth?" he asked me. "I was thinking of other things, I'm afraid, taking advantage of your company. You know, you must learn to put yourself forward more, or nobody will ever notice you, quiet in your corner. You'll never make heads turn, but you do have a great deal of character. You could use that to advantage, to make up—Now I've hurt your feelings, and I didn't mean to. But you'll need a thicker skin for life, my dear. But I'm forgetting— sometimes I'm so selfish I appall even myself," and he smiled at me affectionately. "You've been ill, didn't you say? And you were troubled. Have I diverted you from your troubles, at least a little bit?"

I turned back from where I stood at the stream's edge. "Yes," I said, hearing the surprise in my own voice. He sat watching me, amusement on his face.

"Then I've succeeded, haven't I? It's exactly what I hoped. I've been a comfort, which is just what you needed."

By the time I crossed the stream he had risen and gone.

Chapter Fourteen

I lingered over my stockings and shoes so that I would be sure to be alone as I made my way back down by the brook. Mr. Callender *had* succeeded in diverting me and perhaps it was for that reason that he told me his long story. The story saddened me, not because I felt sorry for him but because of the man he revealed himself to be. That a man could speak so fair and be so fair, yet not be honest, nor even kind, I now suspected; that I found distressing. Also distressing was the question he raised in my mind: if a man lied, then owned that he lied, was he still lying in quite the same way? If a man said frankly that he did not care to be good, was he deceptive? Poor Irene Thiel, I thought, who had spent all her life caring for her brother. No wonder she had been attracted to Mr. Thiel, who, for all his drawbacks, was at least completely honest. Or had she been deceived in Mr.

Thiel too, I wondered, had she been as cruelly disappointed in her husband as she must have been in her brother?

I thought then of Aunt Constance, of her cool and thoughtful presence. Irene Thiel should never have married. She should have lived with Aunt Constance and worked with her, as I had; then at least she might have had some peace.

By the time I reached the glade by the falls, I was properly angry at both of those men. I stumped along the path, my eyes on the ground. That she had been devoted to her husband I felt sure. But whether he had loved her in return, I doubted. I doubted whether he could even feel affection. My footsteps thumped in my ears.

Mac waited for me just down the path. "He told me to fetch you back. Where'd you go?"

"To see Mr. Callender."

"Why?"

I didn't know the answer to that so I did not reply.

"You better hurry," Mac warned me.

I did not increase my speed.

Mr. Thiel waited for us in the library. He stood before the fireplace. His dark face was made darker by anger. He didn't give either Mac or me a chance to speak. He addressed himself only to me.

"You will of course return to Cambridge," he said. The words were cold, but his anger was hot. I could feel the force of it. "Until you are out of my care, you are to stay in this house. Is that understood? You will return to Miss Wainwright on the Friday train. I will telegraph your aunt tomorrow."

I just stared at him. He had no right to talk to me like that. His employee I might be, but I was not his creature. I would not obey him unless I chose to; but I would not stoop to a lie. I kept my mouth firmly shut. He could not force me to answer. Also, I'll admit it, I didn't have the courage to argue with him.

"But sir—" Mac said.

Mr. Thiel turned on him. "And you, young man, will keep yourself off this property until Jean has left. I don't blame you. However, I can't feel that at this time you are a good influence on her. She will get into less mischief alone. Do you give me your word?"

"Yes sir," Mac said. His voice sounded shaky, but he held himself straight enough.

I walked Mac to the front door. "He sure gets angry," Mac said, letting his breath out as soon as we were in the hallway, out of Mr. Thiel's sight. "I thought my dad's lecturing was bad, but this . . ." He shook his head and then grinned at me. "He sure gets angry," he said again.

"I don't care," I said. "So do I."

"What a pair you two are," Mac remarked. "I don't see how you lasted in the same house this long." His grin had not faded, and I began to see the humor of it myself. The two of us, dark and stubborn, both furiously angry. I knew the complex reasons for my own anger, my distress at the hopelessness of Mr. Callender's character, my sense of the way the two men had taken advantage of Irene Thiel's nature, my anger that Mr. Thiel should speak to me so, and beneath it all the fear that blew about me like a dark wind, fear for myself. But what right had Mr. Thiel to be so angry. All he had to do was dismiss me as an unsatisfactory employee.

Dinner that night started off in uncomfortable silence. We ate trout, with potatoes and green beans from Mrs. Bywall's garden. The only sound was the clatter of knives and forks on china. I barely glanced at my employer. Had I been older I would have asked for dinner on a tray in my room.

At last Mr. Thiel broke the silence. "I did not think your aunt would have rasied a sullen child."

I could not judge his tone, so looked at his face. I could not judge his face. I went back to my food.

"I am sorry you have not been happy here," he said, the anger back in his voice.

"It matters little. I've done the work asked of me."

"Yes, you have," he said, as if the admission pained him.

"Perhaps you would prefer me to spend my remaining time in Marlborough elsewhere," I suggested. "I might go over to the Callenders' until it is time for me to leave."

"You'll do no such thing—I forbid it," he said.

I lay down my utensils silently. I looked silently at him.

"Haven't you thought that it was probably there that you ate poison?" he demanded. "Can you be so careless and unthinking, child?"

That he should accuse me of being unthinking was the final straw. But I sounded calm enough, I heard with pleasure how cool my voice was. "No, sir, it seemed just as likely that I might have been given poison here. I have, as you might guess, thought rather carefully on the question—if I had been given poison at all, of course, which is only a conjecture. No, sir, I am not unthinking, if you will forgive me the self-praise. Since you see fit to accuse me of that, I will tell you what I am thinking right now. I think you are jealous of Mr. Callender."

He laughed, once, sharply, not with any humor. "Jealous? Why should I be jealous of him?"

The man's cold and unsympathetic nature increased my fury. "He is so much that you are not," I pointed out. "He, at least, would not take an ignorant girl and place her into a position of danger with no warning, no warning at all." To my dismay, I heard my voice crack.

Mrs. Bywall removed the dinner plates.

After she had gone, Mr. Thiel spoke. His voice was oddly gentle. "You're right, Jean; I know nothing of children." I looked up in surprise and saw how tired he was. His face looked pale; his eyes were the only signs of life in his face. "You're too young, I expected too much of you. You're right, you're much better off with your Aunt Constance."

His gentleness would have melted me, except for the lie he told. "You're lying," I accused him. I don't know why I should have been so disappointed to catch him out. "You had a child, I know it, even though you keep it like some dark, guilty secret."

His face came alive then. I watched him struggle to control his expression.

"I don't know why you're lying, but you'd better not think you can fool me," I said.

Mrs. Bywall stood by the table, a brown betty in her hands, her face pale and frightened, her eyes riveted to Mr. Thiel's face.

"At least Mr. Callender hired detectives, at least he tried," I continued. "You didn't do anything." I waited to hear what the man had to say in his own defense.

But Mr. Thiel simply glared at me from across the table.

"Sir," Mrs. Bywall said, "don't you—"

"Silence!" he roared. "Take that thing back into the kitchen. Not a word. We'll eat it tomorrow."

Despite her fear she tried again. "But sir—" I knew now who was the puppetmaster Mrs. Bywall obeyed, although I did not know why.

"Not a word." He cut her off. "Miss—Wainwright will be leaving us soon. She looks very tired and should probably go right up to bed. A rich dessert will only give her bad dreams."

Once again I left the table, but this time in stony silence. He might have Mrs. Bywall terrified, he might be able to control the tongues of the villagers, he might have broken his wife to his will, but he would not break me. "I'll bid you a good-night," I said from the doorway.

"Good-night." He looked up at me from his seat. He no longer looked angry, only tired. "I'll be gone when you wake up. You're not to leave the house."

I did not answer by gesture or word. He held my eyes with his until I turned away.

As you can imagine, I slipped out of the house the next morning after a breakfast during which Mrs. Bywall resisted all my efforts at conversation. She, poor woman, had no idea that I would disobey Mr. Thiel.

I took a book and went up to the glade by the falls. There I sat on the long grass trying to read. It was a warm, sundrenched morning. The stream rushed over the falls filling the air with its sound. I sat cross-legged in the sunlight and did not open my book.

Recalling our quarrel—I couldn't dignify it with any other name—I was no longer so sure that I had acted as Aunt Constance would have wished. Certainly I had been as disrespectful to my employer as he had to me. Moreover, however badly he had acted, that did not excuse my own ill behavior. Especially in regard to dragging the child into the quarrel, even as a means of proving that Mr. Callender was in some ways the better man. That, I knew, was inexcusable. I could excuse myself—hadn't Mr. Callender said he alone had tried to trace her—but I owed Mr. Thiel an apology.

A rush of air filled my lungs.

It was an impossible idea.

Then I laughed, a sharp and mirthless sound. And Mr. Callender said I had no imagination.

But in the solitude of the glade and beneath the rushing water, I heard how my laugh echoed the unhappy sound Mr. Thiel had made at dinner, when I had accused him of jealousy.

It was a ridiculous idea.

I had to think carefully, very carefully, because if I was correct, everything made sense. I was sure Mr. Callender said he had tried to trace *her*. A girl.

Irene Thiel had said her child would be safe. What safer place than with her old friend, Constance Wainwright? How the nurse had managed to get the child there, I couldn't guess. I could guess at the age, however, since Irene Thiel had been married for four years, and the child had been getting big, as Mr. Callender told me: the child was probably born in 1881 or 1882, and would now be almost thirteen.

As I was. But I had no memory of a witchlike figure; although I did have a shrouded, dark figure in my dreams.

J: Janet or Jessica. Or Jean. I had never thought of that.

Aunt Constance said I was a babe in arms when she got me. For how long could a child be considered a babe in arms? It was impossible. Except that Mr. Callender had guessed my name, which was at least as impossible. He had guessed it in a game he had set up, which was certainly ridiculous—unless my age and my appearance made him suspect. Certainly it explained not only his flattering behavior toward me, but also the trouble to which he had put his family on my account. If I was Irene Thiel's daughter. If Mr. Thiel, for whom he harbored such a bitter dislike was—

I couldn't, even in my mind, say the word.

But if that were true, why would Aunt Constance have let me come up to Marlborough? And why should Mr. Thiel have asked for me? And why should somebody try to poison me? Of course, thinking carefully, I realized that unless I were in Marlborough it would be difficult to get rid of me; if somebody wanted to. Because if I was Irene Thiel's daughter—and she was my mother—then I had inherited the Callender fortune.

I determined to ask Aunt Constance outright when I

returned to Cambridge. I could, I knew, have asked Mr. Thiel. But if he was my—father—and he had chosen not to say anything about that, then he had tricked me into coming to Marlborough after having given me up for years; and I didn't want to make him admit to being my father, if he didn't want to claim me.

Who was it, I wondered, who wanted the Callender fortune badly enough to murder Irene Thiel? Her brother Enoch—but he loved her. Her husband—but he profited most if the child was never identified. Or if the child was dead. Joseph? Victoria? Benjamin? Was their dislike of me, which I had attributed to jealousy over their father's favor, based on knowing I had what they so badly wanted?

But I didn't have it. I didn't even want it. I wanted to belong to Aunt Constance, tied close by the bonds loving years had made between us. I didn't want to be the daughter of a man who, as far as I had seen, had no warm and loving feelings toward his wife and child, who shut them absolutely out of his mind. Whatever his reasons for giving me away, I didn't want to be Jean Thiel. Jean Thiel, the name repeated itself in my mind. Jean Thiel.

A voice, outside my inner thoughts called, "Jean Thiel!"

I looked up, startled. Mr. Callender stood on the other side of the falls. He wore a white linen suit and a panama hat. His hands were casually resting in the pockets of his trousers, as if he were about to begin a stroll down a city street. The blue of his eyes was visible across the distance, so intensely did he look into my face.

"I wondered if I had given it all away, old Dan's little game. Did you know it all along?"

"Know what?" I stood up.

"You can't fool me, Jean Thiel. No, don't run away, it's time we had an honest talk. I know that expression. It's one I've seen often enough on your mother's face. You won't run away from me, will you? You don't have to run away from *me*."

He turned around to get the board down from its hiding place. His hat fell off and his hair shone in the sunlight. He carried the board over to the stream and gently lowered it, to make a bridge.

I watched mesmerized. I wanted to run, but could not. I could not believe he would have killed his sister. I went to stand by the board: if he started to cross over I would lift it aside and prevent him. I would trust nobody. "Stay there," I called.

"You can trust me," he called back. "Think about it, it's obvious you have the intelligence to figure out what's been going on. He won't get away with it, I promise you. I won't let him. I won't sit quiet and wait for his move, not this time."

"How long have you known?" It is odd how once you have hit on the truth, however shocking it may be, you accept it entirely.

"Since the first day I saw you up here. You didn't see me. You're very like her, your mother. I couldn't miss that. Old Dan couldn't have known how like you are, could he? How it would give his game away. And then, you don't know Dan Thiel; he's not the man to take an interest in a school for girls without some personal reason. When you so obligingly told me all about yourself, you confirmed my opinion. I wasted money on those detectives. I should have risked finding you myself, years ago."

"Why?"

"You're too intelligent to need that question answered," he called.

"Money," I answered myself. "But you haven't been poor."

"Say I've been poorer than I should, by right, have been.

But this yelling is ridiculous." He lifted a booted foot to step across.

"Stay over there," I said. I bent down to hold the other end of the board in my hands. He stared at me for a minute, then shrugged his shoulders and smiled. "As you wish. Let me ask you, how long have *you* known?"

"Just now, I just figured it out; I wasn't even sure," I told him.

"Then you're not as clever as I had thought. You're remarkably like your mother, intelligent up to a point and then you let your feelings take over. You should guard against that, my dear. Look where it got your mother."

"What do you mean by that?"

"Everything was fine until she married Dan Thiel. Father was old, he was bound to die soon. I knew that. I asked her to leave Dan and bring you, of course, and we could live as we had before. I would take care of you both, but not her husband. Father had shown me the will, I think he hoped I would mend my ways. She knew Dan would be all right— but he had taken her away from me and she wouldn't even admit that. She was blind."

He moved quickly forward and I lifted the board just off the ground, then I dropped it when I saw him fall. He curled up on the ground, clutching his ankle. His shoulders hunched in. His face was twisted with pain. Both of his hands were wrapped around his ankle.

"What have you done?" he groaned. This time his voice cut under the rushing sound of water.

"I'll get help, it won't be long. I'm sorry. I didn't mean to."

"Not that way, get my *wife*—Joseph can run to the doctor's faster than you can. Jean, *please*." Pain was in his voice, try as he would to disguise it.

He was right, I knew. Mr. Thiel was not at home, he had taken the carriage. I stepped out onto the board, going as fast as I could without risking losing my balance. I kept my eyes down on my bare feet.

And that was why it wasn't until I felt the board move under me that I saw Mr. Callender, erect now, and smiling at me. He stood at the other end. "Just like your mother," he told me. "I ask you, how can a man in stiff boots twist his ankle?"

I put my chin up and did not show how frightened I was. I tried to think carefully: I was younger than Irene Thiel, lighter; I might survive the fall better than she had. Unbidden, I looked down to the boulders below, where water swirled. The weather is warmer than it was then, I told myself, trying not to ask myself how long it would be before I was missed, before Mr. Thiel returned from sending the telegram. Or Mac, if he came to visit—but Mac had given his word to stay off the property.

At that memory, I thought angrily to myself that it would serve Mr. Thiel right.

"Or maybe not so like," Mr. Callender said. "There is something of your father in you, isn't there. Something of his hardness. Do you know what Irene told me? She said"—he laughed as if the idea was preposterous—"that I was trying to force her to choose between us, between Dan and me. Well, what is there to choose? I asked her that. She didn't answer me." He stepped out along the board, approaching.

"Then, I don't know, I thought I'd scare her. Women are so easy to scare. Priscilla is. So I jumped on the board. 'Enoch, stop that,' she said, just like when I was little. But I wasn't little any more. Once again, and she fell. It was dark. I couldn't see. I called to her and she didn't answer. What would you have thought? I thought she was dead. It was an accident, it was all an accident, don't you see?"

At that moment I couldn't see anything, for the tears that were rolling down my cheeks. "You knew where she was?

All the time you knew, when everybody was looking. You were looking too. . . ."

"I thought she was dead. You're sensible, think of it from my side. I thought she was dead, how could I know she wasn't? Then, according to the will, I would inherit at least half. But if I was the one to find her—in this unlikely spot—who would believe I had nothing to do with it? I couldn't be the one to find her. Later, when I heard she hadn't been dead—it was terrible for me."

He looked as if he meant that.

"They said she could have lived. But by then it was too late. How could I have known? Could anyone have known? It's not as if I wanted to kill her. If she had just answered me, I'd have saved her. She loved me."

I felt pity for him then, for what he might have been. And I hated him, at the same time, for what he had done. And I was frightened of him, for what he might do.

"That's just how she looked, Irene, the last time," he said. There was no emotion in his voice, no laughter, no grief. Nothing there at all. "Come home with me now, Jean. We'll be happy. We'll move to New York, or if you prefer we'll travel. You'll be just like one of my own children. I'll take care of you." He stepped along toward me, one hand held out to me.

Instinctively, I stepped back. He moved forward again, out over the falls. Graceful and handsome as a circus acrobat, he came closer. I did not have the will or courage I needed.

The board gave way slightly under my feet, then bounded up again. He held my eyes with his. He smiled into my eyes. "It's the fittest who survive," he told me gently. "Every time."

The board moved again and my arms flew out to give me any kind of balance.

A harsh and ugly sound cracked through the silence, like

the snapping of a whip. A voice, that said my name, angry, demanding obedience. "Jean! Turn—now!"

Mr. Callender looked into the glade behind me, his eyes burning.

"Now! Jump!" the voice ordered.

I turned and jumped. My bare feet touched down on the board before I was flung off toward the edge of the ravine. It was too far for a clear leap, but two strong hands grabbed my wrists painfully and dragged me up to the edge of the clearing. I looked back over my shoulder to see Mr. Callender, gleaming gold and white in the sunlight, trying to balance on the board, which rocked from my own leap. He fell. The board spun down after him.

Chapter Fifteen

Mr. Thiel held me there, in his arms, until I stopped
trembling. "Are you all right?" he asked, as his hands
stroked my head. "You're all right now. You can stop that
wailing. I should have told you, I admit it. Child, child,
you're safe now."

"He killed her," I said.

"I know," Mr. Thiel said, impatient.

"He didn't mean to," I said. I don't know how he could
hear what I was saying, for the strength with which I was
holding on to him, my face buried in his coat.

"I thought not," Mr. Thiel said. "He did love her."

"You're my father," I said.

"Yes, I am," he said. A laugh rumbled in his chest.
"Wasn't that painfully obvious at dinner last night?"

"Daniel?" A voice I knew, Aunt Constance's voice,
spoke breathlessly from behind Mr. Thiel's head. "Some-

body had better look to Enoch. He moves, but seems unable to speak."

I sat up then. Aunt Constance showed the ravages of a run uphill through the woods. "Aunt Constance," I said in surprise. She stooped under the branches as she ran, and her cloak outlined her bent figure.

"You've been foolish," she said to me. Her breath came in gasps as she straightened up, one hand against her heart. "I'm very glad to see you. But Daniel, hadn't you better look to Enoch?"

"Yes," he said. We both stood up. Aunt Constance kept me by her side while he climbed down to the stream. "Better not to look," she said.

"What are *you* doing here?" I asked. I was not, I know, thinking clearly.

"As soon as I received Daniel's last letter I came out," she said. "I'd been worried. I hired a carriage at North Adams this morning, and we met on the road. Otherwise . . ."

That, I could not think of yet.

"Enoch can move his arms but not his legs, apparently," Mr. Thiel, my father, reported. "He can't seem to speak. I'll fetch Dr. McWilliams. It's probably better not to move him until we know what is wrong. I'll go on down, if that's all right?"

Aunt Constance approved of the plan. Mr. Thiel, my father, looked at me. I smiled slightly at him, unexpectedly shy.

"Yes. Well. That's good enough," he said, briefly, clumsily, but it seemed to me happily. "Perhaps better than I should expect. Can you two wait here? He shouldn't be left alone."

We stood, the three of us, in the glade. Aunt Constance protectively bent over me, held one of my hands. Mr. Thiel put his hands on my shoulders. I stood between them, unable to think clearly.

With a stumbling noise, like a deer breaking cover, Mac appeared across the falls. He looked briefly over at us then ran on, slightly upstream. He charged into the water. "Hey!" he yelled across, splashing wildly. "You better not do that!" he yelled.

We stood amazed. Aunt Constance bent toward me. Mac pushed his way through water up to his thighs. He had cuts on his face, his shirt was ripped. He pulled himself up onto the bank and hurtled toward us. With his head lowered, he slammed into Mr. Thiel, my father, forcing him backward.

"Let her go!" Mac said, breathless. He raised his fists. Mr. Thiel—my father—grabbed at his hands and spun Mac around until his arms were crossed across his chest. Mac struggled with his feet to free himself. "Jean!" he panted. "Do something, you can get away from her, she's too old to run, get to our house. Tell my father. Jean!" he urged me. "Tell him the nurse is back, he'll know what to do. Go on!"

I burst out laughing. I knew I shouldn't, but I couldn't help it. Mac stopped struggling and looked over his shoulder at my father.

"May I ask who is this—friend of yours?" Aunt Constance asked me. She stood up again and pushed her hood off her head. Mac's jaw fell.

"Oliver McWilliams, better known as Mac. Let me introduce Miss Constance Wainwright," I said.

Mac's face turned beet red. "You can let me go now, sir," he said. "I seem to have—made a mistake."

"But for good reasons," my father, Mr. Thiel, told him. His dark eyes were laughing, but he did not allow the rest of his face to reveal that. "If I understand your curious attack correctly, you were trying to protect my daughter."

"What happened to your face, Mac?" I asked.

"I had a run-in with Joseph," he told me. His eyes

gleamed. "I found out, Dad told me, they *had* been sick; Mrs. Callender finally came down to fetch him but she had to wait until her husband was out of the house. She was worried about her children, they'd all been ill, and so had she. But Mr. Callender told her not to call the doctor. *He* hadn't been sick, of course. I came to warn you. But I'd given my word to stay off your property, sir." He tugged the ripped sleeve of his shirt, looking proud. "Joseph tried to stop me."

Then his mouth fell open again. "Your daughter?"

"I do have to go, to get your father, and you'd better come down to the house and put on dry clothes. I'll explain on the way. Mr. Callender has had an accident," he explained. He turned Mac by the shoulder, and Mac obeyed without protest, but he asked again as they moved out of earshot, "Your daughter?"

When we were alone, Aunt Constance stood back of me, studying me. Then she hugged me, once, hard, and let me go again. We sat down facing each other. Aunt Constance looked tired, but at ease. "I don't know where to begin," she said.

At a sudden thought I interrupted her. "You were the nurse, the one who disappeared!" I cried.

Her smile lit her face in the way I remembered so well. "Of course. Your mother had asked me to take you, if Daniel thought it best. If anything happened to her."

"Did she know?"

"About Enoch? I think so. She would never admit it, of course. She didn't care so much for herself, I think, but you—she cared for you. She knew Enoch well. She must have known more of what he was capable of than the rest of us suspected. At first, after her death, Daniel thought he could stay in Marlborough and keep you with him. But there were a couple of occasions when odd things happened. There was even a snake once, that somehow got into your crib, or your toy box." She hesitated before going on, remembering something I could not guess at. "He wrote to ask me to come up, as secretly as possible. I came at night, cloaked. We talked it over, and determined that the best thing was for you to disappear."

"Why?"

"You were in danger. I *am* your godmother, you know."

"No, I didn't. How could I?"

She smiled again. "I am, even so. We had no choice, if you think of it. If he could have, Daniel would have given everything to Enoch and supported you himself. Then you would have been safe. But he couldn't. The will gave him no power to disburse the fortune. He wasn't sure what you would want, when you grew up. You are a rich child, you know."

"Am I?" That wasn't important. "Tell me what happened."

"Daniel and I decided that the best possible thing was for everything to be in a sort of limbo, until you were old enough. So for a few weeks, I acted the part of a nurse. That way, one of us was always with you. One night, he drove me to Worcester. You traveled in a basket, sleeping. I walked into the railway station that morning carrying only what seemed to be a rather large picnic for a single lady, and we arrived back in Boston that afternoon. Miss Constance Wainwright and a two-year-old orphan whom she had agreed to raise."

"And nobody here would have known that he had even left the house," I said, "because there would have been nobody in the house to know."

"Yes," she said.

"Mr. Callender hired detectives."

"We thought he might. We weren't sure of it."

"Why didn't you tell me before I came here?" I asked.

"I thought of it. Daniel didn't want me to."

"Why not?"

"He can probably tell you better than I," Aunt Constance protested.

"No, I doubt that," I contradicted.

"Perhaps you're right," she said, after a long thoughtful hesitation. "He didn't know you, remember, not as I do. I think, perhaps, he was afraid of the power of money, and he didn't want you to be told until he was certain it wouldn't corrupt you."

"Like Mr. Callender?"

"Yes. Also—although this is only my suspicion, he's never said anything about this to me—he wanted to know if you could like him, for himself. He isn't the easiest man, and if you disliked him he didn't want to force himself on you. He said it wouldn't be fair to you if I told you before you came here. But I wasn't sure. You weren't very old, after all. I didn't want to let you go."

"I'm old enough," I said.

"I hope so," she answered. "When you wrote, and he wrote, that you were seeing so much of Enoch—I can't tell you how I worried."

"He never forbade it."

"Of course not. He wanted you to choose freely."

"That wasn't very sensible—considering what he knew," I pointed out.

"Perhaps not," Aunt Constance answered. "I suspect he needed to be sure of you. He has his pride."

"Oh!" I said, impatiently. Then, as I thought of how poorly I had managed, even though I had in the end not been deceived by Mr. Callender, I understood with Mr. Thiel had tried to do. And after that, I realized something else: "It's my fault."

"What is?" Aunt Constance was listening to the woods. "It's so peaceful here, isn't it? I always loved the mountains. What's your fault, my love?"

"Mr. Callender. I did to him just what he did to her."

Aunt Constance looked at me sternly. "No," she said. "No, you did not. Think carefully for a minute."

"I didn't mean to hurt him. But he said he didn't mean to hurt his sister," I protested.

"Can you believe him?" Aunt Constance asked gently. "I never thought he really knew what he was doing, just as nobody could ever be sure of what he would do. Enoch never considered consequences. I suspect that he chose to do just what he did do, but could not tell even himself the truth. Think, Jean."

I thought. "I see," I said. "Still, I am responsible."

"For the consequences, yes, I think you are. But you are not guilty. We will talk to your father about it, shall we?"

"My father," I said. "How strange."

"You'll get used to it." Aunt Constance took my hand. "Your mother loved him dearly."

"I know," I said. But had he so loved her, I wondered. Or his child, me. He had, after all, it seemed, protected me after his own fashion. But I had, I knew, seen nothing of his heart; I could not deceive myself about that.

For a long time nothing happened. We sat silent together. Aunt Constance went occasionally to the edge of the falls to be sure that nothing had changed down there. I did not look. I could not. Aunt Constance assured me there was no need. "He hasn't moved. His body is mostly out of the water. He knows we are here and that Daniel will bring help. There is nothing you can do."

She talked quietly to me. She told me about her friend, my mother. I spoke a little about the work I had done on the papers. When I started to tell her about the last week, all the events crowding in, she would not let me. "Wait until your mind is clearer. You've had several shocks, Jean. Now you must relax."

After a long time, or what seemed a long time, Mr.

Thiel—my father—called from across the falls. "Constance? Jean? The doctor is down with Enoch now. Mrs. Bywall expects you at the house for luncheon. Mac is waiting there. Impatiently."

As we turned to go, I saw Mr. Callender's family approaching. Victoria had her arm around her mother. Benjamin was first, striding ahead. Joseph looked as if he had been rolling in dirt. It is the last I have seen of them.

Back at the house, we all sat down to luncheon, Mrs. Bywall included. Mac wore a pair of men's overalls and his face had been washed.

"It's all right, Miss, isn't it?" Mrs. Bywall asked Aunt Constance, who nodded yes. "I've been that worried." To me, she said, "If I'd known what you were thinking about . . . well, I'd have told you some things. Mr. Thiel told me I wasn't to gossip to you, so I didn't, of course, but if I'd known, I'd have gone ahead, whatever he said. When I think . . . Is it true? Are you the little girl?"

"Yes," I said. I couldn't say any more.

"Imagaine that," she said. "Imagine. I can't imagine it."

"What happened?" Mac asked me.

"Aunt Constance was the nurse," I told him. I admit, I said it smugly. "The old, wrinkled witch," I reminded him.

"I *told* you that was only gossip."

"And why didn't you come up through Mr. Thiel's, through my father's property. It was important enough, you should have known that. If Aunt Constance hadn't taken the night train—and met him on the road—and you were busy tussling with Joseph—"

Mac opened his mouth to argue, then shut it. "You're right. It wasn't smart of me. I was a fool."

His simple honesty made me ashamed of myself. "There were two of us."

"What do you mean?"

"Me," I admitted.

"Did you go out on that board again?" Mac demanded.

"He did too."

"You ninny!"

"How was I to know?" I defended myself. "He pretended he'd hurt his ankle, I thought he needed help. How could I tell he was just pretending?"

"I told you he's a snake," Mac reminded me.

"It seems to me," Aunt Constance said peacefully, "that neither of you have behaved with good sense. So perhaps we should let that matter drop."

It was a relief to be where Aunt Constance would correct me in her schoolroom voice. Nothing could have shown me as clearly as that how chaotic the last days had been.

"Is he dead?" Mac asked. Mrs. Bywall gasped and put her hand over mine.

"No," Aunt Constance said. "Injured badly, I suspect, but not dead." Then she surprised me utterly by putting her head down on her hands and weeping.

"Don't do that, Aunt Constance," I said. "Please don't cry."

"Hush you now, let her," Mrs. Bywall said. "You two have been enough to make anyone cry."

Aunt Constance raised her head and smiled. "It's not only that, thank you," she said. She blew her nose on her handkerchief and continued to weep as she spoke. "I've been so worried, all summer long. And it brings the past back so clearly."

"Tears clear the air," Mrs. Bywall announced. "And a pot of tea after, to settle the spirits. Mr. Thiel won't be back for a while is what I'm thinking. I'll keep him a lunch. It will give me something to do with my hands. You might want to wait in the library. I've built a fire, I don't know why, but the house seemed so cold to me this morning, and I

177

couldn't think of anything else to do. A nice fire, a nice pot of tea."

"Would you excuse me for a moment?" I asked Aunt Constance's permission.

"Aren't you going to tell us what happened?" Mac asked.

"I will, I promise, but in a little while. There's something I want to see," I explained to Aunt Constance.

She looked at me puzzled. I couldn't say more. At last, she nodded her head. "Mac and I will wait for you in the library. Perhaps Mac might like to show me how far he has come with Latin."

Mac groaned, then caught her eye and agreed. "We haven't done much for the last few days," he said.

"Never make excuses," Aunt Constance advised him.

I slipped through the kitchen and out the back door. I crossed the garden and went over to the studio. What I was looking for, precisely, I did not know. I knew only that I needed some glimpse into Mr. Thiel's heart, into my father's heart. I knew, by then, the external man, knew also that I could not expect him to change. But I wanted to see into him, to know whether the true man had been revealed by my mother's words in her affectionate note, or by Mr. Callender's tales of him. That Mr. Callender had lied, I was aware; but he had not lied about everything. If I was to be Jean Thiel and not Jean Wainwright—surely I would have something to say in the matter—I wanted to know the real nature of the man who was my father. I thought that I would be more likely to see that in his paintings than anywhere else.

I saw it as soon as I stepped through the door: a large oil painting hung where it dominated the bright room—a portrait of a woman and a child. The child was learning to walk, the woman's arms were held out to her. They were at the glade by the falls, and behind them the beeches seemed to sway in a gentle wind, beyond them the mountains circled protectively. Out of a clear sky, sunlight washed down over them, in benediction. The dark-eyed child, the dark-haired woman, they leaned toward one another; I could almost hear the woman's soft laughter. The scene had caught a moment of movement, so that it could not have been painted from life. The child's foot was raised off the ground, and she might tumble over or step successfully. Either one was possible. It was a portrait done from memory, and in every line, in every brush stroke, in every tiny detail, the painter's heart was visible.

I stood before it, and I wept. Whether from joy, sorrow, or simple admiration, I could not say.

My father stood suddenly beside me. He passed me a handkerchief. "Blow your nose," he instructed me.

"You told me you didn't paint portraits," I said to him.

"I told you, if you remember, that I didn't paint what I didn't understand," he corrected me. "Children are relatively simple to understand."

"I'm *not* a child," I reminded him.

He looked at me without answering.

"And she isn't." I indicated the woman in the portrait.

"No," he agreed.

I looked up at him in surprise: had I made my point so easily? His dark eyes studied me. For a long time we looked at one another so. At last, "All right, in some respects I am a child," I admitted. "But I am twelve, almost thirteen."

"Yes," he agreed. "I couldn't paint you now."

"Of course," I said, "at some later date you might want to."

That caused him to smile, and I had to smile back at him. We turned to go into the house, where there was so much that needed settling.

Chapter Sixteen

What is left to tell? All the important things are left, it seems. What is important changes when the disastrous events have completed themselves. Or maybe Aunt Constance is right, that it is the consequences of what you do that matter most.

Mr. Callender, my uncle, never spoke again. The doctors said there was no reason for his loss of speech, no medical reason. He could have spoken, had he wanted to, but he refused. Perhaps it was because he could no longer move his legs and so he sullenly refused to help himself in any way. Perhaps it was because he had hoped for so much, gambled for it and then lost. He was confined to a wheelchair. Dr. McWilliams said he always would be, until he died. The specialists in Boston agreed, as did those in London and Vienna. As I said, I never saw any of them again, but my father and I have taken care of them.

When Mr. Callender was well enough, he and his family

journeyed to Europe. They live now at a small hotel in Germany, near an Alpine spa, the mineral waters of which are supposed sometimes to produce miracles. We send money to Mrs. Callender, more than enough, through a bank in Munich. She writes once or twice a year, to say all is well with them. Joseph has become responsible for the family and manages the properties they decided to purchase with their half of the Callender estate. Victoria attends concerts and balls and has several suitors. Benjamin has been apprenticed to a bank in Munich. With each letter, Mrs. Callender sounds clearer in mind, happier, stronger. One letter, sent over a year and a half after the accident, closed with a strange remark. The second accident at the bridge, she said, had been the first good thing to happen for her family.

She is right, I think. I can see it now, although I couldn't at the time. Mr. Callender's presence was like a distorting mirror to his children and his wife. He twisted them, somehow, altered them. He was like a dark cloud holding them in its shadow. They were all afraid of him, especially his wife. When he became helpless, they all emerged into a kind of sunlight. Mrs. Callender more and more returned to the character she must once have had, not particularly clever or able, but kind and generous and loving. Although she keeps the children from him, she will never leave him. She loves him. Even now, I can understand that.

Mac has learned to pass Latin and has decided to study medicine when he finishes Harvard. He has not changed, except to grow taller. His voice is deeper. He is still a little wild at heart and probably always will be.

I have not grown accustomed to being an heiress. My father says he hopes I never will. At the end of that summer, Aunt Constance and I returned to Cambridge. My father moved there during the winter. I lived with him then, but missed my life at the school. I missed the little girls, my garden, my Saturday walks, and the quiet conversations in

Aunt Constance's study. I missed the close companionship of my aunt. We did not live far from the school, and I continued my attendance there, so I wasn't separated from her. And I did enjoy the new life I was leading, the new companionship with my father. It is, sometimes, as if he and I have always been together, as if those ten years apart lasted no more than a day. Sometimes, of course, when one or the other of us has been especially cross or difficult, I catch him looking at me as if the ten years' separation was not nearly long enough. I know I sometimes look at him that way—sometimes. He paints, and his fame grows. We go back to the Berkshires each summer. I have grown accustomed to him, and he has grown accustomed to me. We do well together, as Mrs. Bywall says. She has reason to know, because she keeps both houses for him.

The most important consequence took the longest to bring about. I don't know why it wasn't as clear to them as it was to me what should be done. But Aunt Constance always believes in thinking carefully about things. My father finally persuaded her to marry him, which had always seemed to me the obvious step. When I chide either of them with this, they remind me that I am a child and do not understand everything. I suspect I understand more than they think, but do not tell them that. For instance, I suspect that Aunt Constance was afraid he would ask her to give up the school, which he would never dream of doing. He does not want a dependent female making demands on him. I also suspect that she was embarrassed, after so many years of proud spinsterhood, to marry at all.

My father persevered, as he puts it, cautiously and carefully. When I told him, that first winter we spent together in Cambridge, that she had once said they were two of a kind, he first roared with laughter and then fell silent. "I see," he said. I think he did see. We think alike, my father and I.

About the Author

Cynthia Voigt was raised in Connecticut and graduated from Dana Hall School and Smith College in Massachusetts. For a number of years she was a teacher of English and classics, and before that she worked at "various jobs in various states."

She lives in Annapolis, Maryland, with her husband, their two children, and the family dog. In addition to writing and teaching (to which she has recently returned), she enjoys cooking, eating, crabbing, and family summers on an island in Chesapeake Bay.

Mrs. Voigt's first novel, HOMECOMING, was nominated in 1982 for the American Book Award. DICEY'S SONG, a sequel to HOMECOMING, won the Newbery Medal in 1983. She has also written TELL ME IF THE LOVERS ARE LOSERS.

In The Winner's Circle
CYNTHIA VOIGT

Dicey, James, Maybeth and Sammy found themselves abandoned and stranded in an unknown town, and it seemed that every grown-up in the country was against them. Dicey, the oldest, knew she had to keep the children together. Under Dicey's guidance, the children begin a remarkable journey from Connecticut to Maryland in search of their grandmother and love.

77089 $2.25

1983 Newbery Medal winner and sequel to HOMECOMING. Dicey and the children have found the grandmother they had never known and hope their troubles will be over. But old problems and feelings did not go away easy, especially for Dicey, who could not forget about their mother. In the end it takes a crisis for Dicey to accept and begin to enjoy her new life.

70071 $2.25

Confronting
the real issues
in a
realistic way...

JUNIPER BOOKS